PINING AWAY

"We think Belle misses Stevie," Carole said, shooting Stevie's brother Chad a dirty look. *And it's all your fault,* she thought but didn't say.

"Horses have very delicate digestive systems," Lisa said. "Any little thing can throw them off . . ." She let her voice fade away and looked to Carole for support.

"It can be very serious," Carole said.

"Very," Lisa whispered.

"Oh, come off it," Chad said. "Give me a break, will you?" He picked up his soccer ball and bounced it a few times. "You expect me to believe that Stevie's horse is sick because it misses her? I've been around horses, too, you know, and they aren't that smart. Plus, Belle weighs, like, a thousand pounds. She could not eat for a month and be okay." He looked sideways at Lisa. "You guys made this up, right? Did Stevie put you up to it?"

Lisa maintained her earnest, sorrowful expression. "I wish we were joking," she said.

THE SADDLE CLUB

TIGHT REIN

BONNIE BRYANT

A SKYLARK BOOK
NEW YORK · TORONTO · LONDON · SYDNEY · AUCKLAND

RL 5, 009–012

TIGHT REIN

A Bantam Skylark Book / August 1996

Skylark Books is a registered trademark of Bantam Books, a division of Bantam
Doubleday Dell Publishing Group, Inc. Registered in U.S. Patent and Trademark
Office and elsewhere.

"The Saddle Club" is a registered trademark of Bonnie Bryant Hiller.
The Saddle Club design/logo, which consists of a riding crop and a riding hat,
is a trademark of Bantam Books.

"USPC" and "Pony Club" are registered trademarks of The United States
Pony Clubs, Inc., at The Kentucky Horse Park, 4071 Iron Works Pike,
Lexington, KY 40511-8462.

ISBN 0-553-48370-6

Published simultaneously in the United States and Canada.

Bantam Books are published by Bantam Books, a division of Bantam Doubleday Dell
Publishing Group, Inc. Its trademark, consisting of the words "Bantam Books" and
the portrayal of a rooster, is Registered in U.S. Patent and Trademark Office and in
other countries. Marca Registrada. Bantam Books, 1540 Broadway, New York, New
York 10036.

PRINTED IN THE UNITED STATES OF AMERICA

OPM   0 9 8 7 6 5 4 3 2 1

I would like to express my special thanks
to Kimberly Brubaker Bradley
for her help in the writing of this book.

TIGHT REIN

LISA ATWOOD PAUSED outside the door of Prancer's stall. She took a deep breath and smiled. All her favorite sights, smells, and sounds were right here, at Pine Hollow Stables in the summertime. Lisa loved the warm, earthy smell of horses. She loved the feel of their sleek summer fur. She loved the low whickering noise Prancer made when she first saw Lisa.

"We're a team now, aren't we?" Lisa murmured, stroking the mare's velvet-soft nose. Lisa had not been riding long, but she had learned fast. One of her greatest pleasures was riding and retraining Prancer. The beautiful

Thoroughbred had been a racehorse, and Max Regnery, the owner of Pine Hollow Stables, had bought her when an injury ended her career on the track. At first Prancer had been nervous, excitable, and difficult to ride, but she and Lisa had learned a lot together. Riding Prancer, Lisa thought as she went into the stall and slipped a halter on the mare, was the next best thing to having her own horse.

"Lisa?" Max called. He came down the aisle and stopped outside Prancer's stall. "Lisa, sorry, but I used Prancer in the advanced adult lesson this morning, and it's too hot outside to ask her to work hard again. Why don't you ride Barq today?" He gave her a sympathetic smile. "I'll try to let you ride Prancer on Tuesday, okay?" Lisa and her two best friends took lessons twice a week, Tuesdays and Saturdays. They spent most of their free time at Pine Hollow, too.

"Okay, Max," Lisa said, swallowing her disappointment. She liked to think of Prancer as her own horse, but she knew better. Max had too many students to let them ride only their favorites. She gave Prancer a quick hug, removed her halter, and went down to Barq's stall. He was a chestnut Arabian gelding. His name meant "lightning" in Arabic, and he had a feisty personality to match his name. Lisa knew he was a good horse, and she had ridden him many times, but she had never really gotten along with him. She wasn't excited about riding him. She patted him briefly and began to groom him.

"Hi, Lisa! Why aren't you riding Prancer?"

Lisa looked up and smiled. Carole Hanson, one of her two best friends, smiled back.

"I don't have to ask, do I?" Carole said. "Max probably used her in a lesson already. It's too hot today for her to work again."

"That's exactly what he said," Lisa replied with a shake of her head. Lisa considered herself horse-crazy, but not as horse-crazy as Carole. When it came to horses, Carole seemed to know everything.

Carole crossed the aisle to the stall of her horse, a beautiful bay gelding named Starlight. He had been her Christmas present a couple of years ago. She went into his stall and began to groom him. "Don't be too disappointed, Lisa," she said. "It's good for you to ride different horses sometimes. You learn more."

"I know." Lisa was surprised at the slight edge she heard in her own voice. "I know," she repeated more gently. "I just really wanted to ride Prancer today. I mean, Max is letting me take her to camp. He could have saved her for me today."

"That's probably why he didn't save her," Carole answered. She curried Starlight's coat in sweeping circles. "I don't know how you get so dirty, Starlight, when I brush you every day!" she told her horse. To Lisa, she continued, "No one else'll get to ride Prancer while we're at camp, so I bet Max is letting other people have their turn now."

Lisa had to admit that this made sense. She settled Barq's saddle on his back and reached under his belly for the girth. In exactly one week they would all—Lisa, Carole, and their other best friend, Stevie Lake—be at Moose Hill Riding Camp. Lisa couldn't wait.

The three of them were such good friends and loved riding so much that they called themselves The Saddle Club. The only club rules were that they had to love horses and had to help each other out. The Saddle Club had been to Moose Hill before. This year Carole was bringing Starlight, and Stevie was bringing her mare, Belle. Lisa would have Prancer all to herself for the whole week. She couldn't wait!

"I'm so glad Stevie's head is okay," Lisa said. "What would we do if she couldn't go to camp?" Stevie had suffered a serious concussion in a jumping accident, and she hadn't been allowed to ride for a few weeks. Those had been long weeks for the three girls. Lisa and Carole had still ridden, of course, and when Stevie had healed a bit she'd come to visit Belle, but they'd all missed the long rides they usually took together.

Carole giggled. "I'm glad her concussion's healed,

4

too," she said. "But I'm not sure I'd say her head's okay. Stevie's mind always seems a little odd to me."

Lisa laughed appreciatively. She was logical, she knew, and she usually thought things through. Carole could be absentminded, except when she was thinking about horses, but Stevie—they still hadn't figured out how Stevie's mind worked. Stevie came up with more strange, complicated schemes than any ten other people—and most of the time they worked.

"It's not like Stevie to be late, though," Lisa said. She finished buckling Barq's bridle and checked her watch. "We've got exactly five minutes." Max hated it when his students were late for lessons.

"I'm here!" they heard Stevie shout from the tack room, and a moment later she came out carrying her saddle, bridle, and grooming bucket. Lisa and Carole stared. Stevie had shoulder-length blond hair, and when she rode she usually pulled it into a low ponytail. Unlike the others, who wore old breeches to their lessons, Stevie preferred to ride in worn-out jeans and a pair of battered cowboy boots.

Today, however, Stevie's hair was plastered to her head. The end of her ponytail dripped. Her purple shirt clung to her shoulders, and her jeans were wringing wet. As Stevie came down the aisle, Lisa thought she could hear her sloshing.

5

"What happened?" she asked in dismay.

Stevie dumped her gear on the rack outside Belle's stall. "I'll kill him," she said. She brought Belle out of the stall and tied the horse on cross-ties in the aisle. "I mean it," she said emphatically. "I'm really going to get him this time."

Lisa caught Carole's eye. "Uh-oh," she said.

"So what was it this time?" Carole asked. Neither she nor Lisa had to ask who the "him" was that Stevie was going to get. Stevie had three brothers. Michael, the youngest, was pretty quiet. Alex was Stevie's twin and usually left her alone. Her older brother, Chad, however, loved practical jokes as much as Stevie did—and that was an awful lot.

"He got me with the old water-bucket-over-the-door routine," Stevie sputtered. "Look at me! I'm all wet! And the rest of my clothes are in the laundry, so I couldn't change."

"All your other clothes are dirty?" Lisa asked in amazement. Stevie wasn't known for her extensive wardrobe, but she certainly had more than one pair of old jeans. Lisa tied Barq safely in his stall and began brushing Belle for Stevie. Carole tied up Starlight and started picking the mud from Belle's hooves.

"We-ell," Stevie said as she smoothed the saddle pad across Belle's withers, "this summer I'm supposed to be

6

doing my own laundry, and, you know, I kind of forgot." Her face brightened. "But that's okay. I threw in a humongous load a few minutes ago, just before I left. I put a bunch of Chad's clothes in the washer, too, including his brand-new red T-shirt, and I washed it on hot."

"But that means—" Carole said. She did her own laundry, too. Her mother had died a few years ago, and she and her father divided the household chores.

"That's right," Stevie said with satisfaction. "Everything he owns that was white should be pink by now."

"Isn't that a little extreme?" Carole asked. "I mean, I agree the bucket prank was annoying—you won't be very comfortable riding in wet jeans—but Stevie, Chad could end up with pink underwear!"

"I certainly hope so," Stevie said.

"And didn't you do that to him once already?" Lisa asked jokingly. "It's not like you to be repetitive!" It occurred to Lisa that all Stevie's white clothes that had been in the washer were going to turn pink, too. She decided not to say anything. It would only make Stevie more annoyed with Chad.

"Oh," Stevie said, "but it was worth it this time! See, Chad's supposed to be doing his own laundry, too. So he can't complain to our parents, because then he'd have to admit that he wasn't doing his share. It's perfect!" Stevie unsnapped Belle's halter, slipped it around her neck, and fastened it. It would hold Belle until she could be bridled.

"Trust me," Stevie said. "Pink underwear is not too extreme. I don't care if I wreck *all* Chad's clothes. After everything he's done to me this summer—he and his creepy friend Mark—"

Stevie slid the reins of the bridle over Belle's head. She paused and counted on her fingers. "One, they put whipped cream in my riding boots; two, they replaced the shampoo in my bottle with chocolate syrup—"

"All you need is ice cream," Carole said. "You'd have a sundae!"

"Three," Stevie continued, "they glued the pages of my horse magazine together—*before* I read it—"

"Ouch!" Lisa said. "That's serious!"

"Fourth and most unbelievably," Stevie said, "they hung my underwear from the flagpole the day Phil came over to swim." Phil Marsten was Stevie's boyfriend. He rode, too, and he was going to Moose Hill camp the same week they were.

"Don't forget the popcorn incident," Lisa reminded her.

"That's right!" Stevie shrieked. Lisa flinched. Perhaps

she shouldn't have reminded Stevie—she looked plenty worked up already.

A week earlier Carole and Lisa had spent the night at Stevie's. Chad's friend Mark had been sleeping over with Chad. The Saddle Club had been upstairs in Stevie's bedroom, and Chad and Mark had been in the kitchen making popcorn—lots of popcorn—when the girls suddenly thought they heard scuffling noises outside Stevie's door. Then they definitely heard Chad snicker. Stevie threw open her door, and gallons upon gallons of popped corn poured into the room. The boys had tacked a bedsheet to the doorframe and filled the space in between with popcorn.

It would have been a pretty funny prank, Lisa thought, if it had been played on someone else. Cleaning up all the popcorn had taken ages. There was probably still some under Stevie's bed.

Lisa looked at Carole and shook her head. They'd heard Stevie complain about these pranks before. She'd been annoyed for days. Lisa knew Stevie really couldn't complain to her parents. In the first place, Stevie played more than a few practical jokes herself. In the second place, letting her parents intervene would take away all the fun of revenge.

Stevie shook her head. Her wet ponytail slapped her

cheek, and she pushed it away. "I need a strategy here," she said. "I need a battle plan. I need—"

"—to *hurry,*" Carole cut in.

Stevie laughed. "Definitely. And more than anything, I need to ride." She eased the bit of the bridle into Belle's mouth and pulled the headpiece up toward Belle's ears. Belle tossed her head suddenly, and the bit fell from her mouth.

"Easy, girl," Stevie said soothingly. Again she gave Belle the bit, and again Belle tossed her head when Stevie pulled the rest of the bridle toward Belle's ears. This time Stevie was prepared. She pulled the mare's nose back down gently and carefully settled the headstall. Once the strap was over her ears, Belle seemed to relax.

"What was that about?" Lisa asked. Stevie's horse, like all well-trained horses, was usually very calm about this sort of thing.

"I don't know," Stevie said. She pulled the noseband of the bridle snug against Belle's jaw and started to buckle it. Belle fidgeted and tried to sidestep away. Stevie persisted.

"You know what?" Stevie said. "I think her teeth must hurt. She was a little funny about this yesterday, too. I bet she needs to have her teeth floated."

10

"Probably," Carole agreed.

"Floated?" Lisa asked. "Floated in what?" She noticed Stevie and Carole exchanging a small grin. *Well,* she thought irritably, *it's not my fault they know something I don't. I wasn't born in a stable; I don't know everything about horses yet.*

"Horses' back molars grow continuously," Stevie explained. "When they chew, they grind their teeth down. Unfortunately, a lot of horses grind unevenly, and their teeth develop sharp points. Then it hurts them to have a bridle put on."

"If you let their teeth go too long, it can even hurt them to be ridden or to eat," Carole continued. "Vets file the points down, and that's called floating the horse's teeth. It needs to be done about once a year."

"I see," said Lisa.

"Belle's due," Stevie said. "I'll have to call Judy." Judy Barker was the Pine Hollow veterinarian. Stevie patted Belle's nose. "I think it's just putting the bridle on that hurts; I don't think it hurts her to wear it once it's on," she added. "Carole, do you think it'll make Belle uncomfortable if I ride today?"

Lisa watched Carole thinking the question over and wished that for once in her life she could be the one people asked for horse advice.

11

"I think you can ride," Carole said. "See, the reason it hurts her to be bridled has to do with the anatomy of the horse's jaw—"

"Let's *go*," Lisa snapped. "We're all going to be late. Max is waiting." She could tell that Carole was about to launch into one of her fact-filled lectures, and just now she didn't want to hear it.

Her feelings surprised her. Carole and Stevie were her two best friends! But sometimes, Lisa thought, it got just a little tiresome not knowing as much as they did. She'd never even heard of filing horses' teeth. Lisa knew she was smart, but around the stable she sometimes felt she'd never catch up to Carole and Stevie.

THE RIDING LESSON didn't make Lisa feel any better. After their usual warm-up, Max set them to performing exercises. The idea was to change the length of the stride, not the speed at which the horse moved. First Max set up a grid of poles on the ground about four feet apart, and the riders trotted the horses over them. If the horses moved correctly, their feet wouldn't hit any of the poles.

Then Max pushed the poles closer together. Each rider had to shorten her horse's stride, making it more up-and-down and less forward-moving, or the horse would knock its hooves against the poles. Stevie and

Carole did fine. Veronica diAngelo glided through on her superhorse, Danny. Simon Atherton and Delilah sounded like a pinball machine: *clank! clank! clank!*

Barq, like most Arabs, had no trouble shortening, and Lisa felt proud when they made it through the grid without a single clank.

Then Max spread the poles farther apart. This meant the horses had to stretch their strides out low and long. Barq had become very happy trotting with an up-and-down motion, and he didn't want to change. He set his jaw against the reins and refused to move into a longer stride. Lisa tried urging him forward with her legs, the way Max said, but Barq just trotted short and fast.

Lisa came around the corner toward the pole grid. In front of her, Starlight and Belle swept through effortlessly.

Barq trotted in. *Clank, clank, clank.* He stumbled over the last pole, and Lisa had to grab his mane to keep her balance. She felt her face flush.

"Don't worry, Lisa, this is hard for him," Max said. "Try it again."

But no matter how many times she tried, she couldn't get it. Belle would go through the grid, then Starlight, both beautifully. Barq would whack every rail.

Lisa knew she could have gotten Prancer to lengthen her stride easily. The Thoroughbred would have sailed

13

through this exercise, not staggered and stumbled like short-strided Barq.

If I had my own horse, Lisa thought, *this would be easier.* Lisa was not the youngest member of The Saddle Club, but today she felt as if she were. She knew her feelings weren't Carole and Stevie's fault. It wasn't Carole and Stevie's fault that they had their own horses, either, or that she didn't. Still, she felt miserable.

"NOTHING'S WORSE THAN riding wet," Stevie declared as she unsaddled Belle. "I'm going to get even with Chad. I mean it. Right *now.*"

"You can't get even with him right now," Lisa reminded her. "You guys are coming to my house from here, aren't you?" They had planned a sleepover at Lisa's. "You won't have to worry about Chad there," she told her friend.

"Of course I remembered that we're going to your house," said Stevie. Suddenly she whirled around, almost dropping her saddle and causing Belle to prance on the cross-ties. "Ohmigosh! I just remembered something else! Mark's spending the night at my house, with Chad!"

"While you're at Lisa's you won't have to worry about Mark either," Carole said.

Stevie shook her head. "It's obvious that you two

have no experience with siblings," she said. "Don't you see? Mark and Chad will have the whole night to plan their next attack on me, and I won't be there to stop them!" She shook her head. "We have got to do something," she said. "We can't let him get away with it."

2

"WELL," LISA SAID, suppressing a giggle, "I definitely don't think this is a smart idea." She was standing up to her ankles in one of Mrs. Lake's petunia beds. It was around ten o'clock the same night, and it was cloudy and very dark. To her left, Lisa could see a faint shimmer from the Lakes' swimming pool, as well as several shrouded humps that she guessed were lawn furniture. Shadows lurked around the edges of the fenced yard.

To her right, Lisa couldn't see anything, because she was standing against the side of Stevie's house. Straight

16

ahead she could see Carole, also trying not to laugh, and between them she could see the ladder they were holding steady while Stevie climbed it.

"Definitely not a smart idea," Lisa repeated.

"Shhh!" Stevie said from above.

They had put the ladder directly under the window of Chad's bedroom. Stevie was certain Chad was plotting something evil, and she was determined to know what it was. No stinking older brother was going to take advantage of her!

It was a short walk from Lisa's house to Stevie's. The girls had crept out as soon as it looked really dark. Lisa's parents had been playing bridge with friends in the den, so Lisa was pretty sure they'd never even notice that The Saddle Club was gone.

First the girls had strung toilet paper all over the bushes in front of the house. Eight rolls were all they could come up with on short notice, but they'd made the best of what they had. Stevie had brought her water pistol and sprayed all the TP, making it stick to the bushes like soggy oatmeal so that it would be seventeen times harder to remove. The rule in the Lake house, Stevie had explained, was that if your friends made the mess, you had to clean it up. Since Stevie was staying at Lisa's, she was pretty certain that the blame for this job would rest solely on Chad's friends—and therefore on

Chad. Of course, Alex might catch some of the blame, too, but that was okay.

Stevie had even spelled WE LOVE YOU, CHAD in the middle of the lawn with pink TP. Not only would that be a false clue leading directly to Chad, but it would make Chad think that some girl actually loved him.

While Stevie had decorated the grass, Lisa and Carole had thrown the remaining rolls of toilet paper through the trees, until streamers hung from all the branches and wafted in the breeze. When they were finished, the front of the Lake house looked decidedly festive.

Then they got a ladder from Stevie's father's shed and propped it against the back of the house. Now Stevie was climbing the ladder as quietly as a cat to spy on her brother. She knew he was up to something.

"What if Chad and Mark are in the basement?" Carole whispered. She felt something pricking the backs of her legs. A rosebush, maybe? She knew she was standing on some sort of plant. The smell of crushed petunias hung heavy in the air.

"What if they're making popcorn?" Lisa whispered. She shook with silent laughter. The ladder trembled.

"Shhh!" Stevie hissed. "I can see them! They're in there." Lisa and Carole could hear her take a final step up the ladder. "They're giggling," Stevie murmured. "I don't like it . . . they've got Super Glue. . . ." Sud-

18

denly Stevie's screech tore through the silent night air. *"They've got my riding boots again!"*

Carole and Lisa jumped and nearly dropped the ladder. *"Shhh!"* they said in unison.

Through the window Stevie could see that Chad had spotted her and was laughing. His clammy, troll-like hands were on her beloved new boots. She hammered her fist against the window frame. "Those are mine!" she bellowed. "Mine! Put those down! I'll get you for this, Chad Lake! You won't get away with it this time!"

Inside the house, Chad and Mark guffawed and pointed at Stevie. Stevie tried to open the window, but it was locked from the inside.

"Stevie!" Lisa cried. "Your parents will hear!" Mr. and Mrs. Lake had been watching TV in the living room— the girls had peeked in before starting to TP the lawn. Mr. Lake liked to have the TV loud, but it wouldn't be loud enough to drown out Stevie's bellowing.

"Get down from there!" Carole urged.

"You cretinous, lard-bellied fool!" Stevie shouted. "You miserable, slack-jawed, booger-brained moron!" She pounded the window frame in helpless fury. Inside, Chad and Mark dangled her boots inches from the glass, laughing hysterically.

"C'mon, Stevie! We've got to run for it!"

"Boggy-bottomed, zit-faced toad!"

"*Stevie!*"

Carole and Lisa could see lights coming on inside the house. They were running out of time, but they couldn't leave Stevie on the unsteady ladder.

"Stevie!" Lisa called again.

Stevie finally recognized the peril of their situation. She scurried down the ladder and jumped the last few feet. She stumbled, landing in her mother's small vegetable garden. Ripe tomatoes exploded under her feet. An eggplant squished against her chest. "I'm caught," she said, thrashing among the bean vines and tomato stakes.

"I'll take the ladder—you get Stevie!" Lisa said to Carole. She pulled the ladder down and swung it around. The front end caught on the umbrella table by the swimming pool. Desperately Lisa tried to yank it free.

Carole was on her hands and knees pulling Stevie loose from the garden. When she saw Lisa struggling, she got up and jerked the ladder free. It shot out of her grasp and tore through the mesh on the back screen door.

"Oh, no!"

The porch lights went on. The pool lights went on. The girls dashed around in panic. Carole, fighting to free the ladder from the screen door, lost her footing and fell into the pool. The ladder fell in after her. Lisa screamed.

20

Stevie, still trailing bean vines, tripped over a lawn chair and skidded into the last remaining flower bed.

Above them, they heard wood screech as Chad opened his window. He stuck his head out and blew a raspberry at the girls.

"Stevie! What do you think you're doing!" Mr. and Mrs. Lake rushed out the back door, but Stevie didn't hear them. Sprawled in a bed of crushed pansies, she glared with dark fury at her brother.

"I'm going to kill you, Chad Lake!" she screamed. "I'll get you for this if it's the last thing I do!"

3

"WOW." CAROLE SHOOK HER HEAD dejectedly. "This is just awful. I mean, *awful.*" Beside her, Lisa nodded. Carole slumped against the side of the stable wall. It was Sunday afternoon. The two of them had just met at Pine Hollow, and now they were sitting outside the stable, watching the horses in the pasture grazing in the warm sunshine. It would have been a wonderful day, Carole thought, if they all hadn't been in such big trouble.

"So how mad were your parents?" she asked Lisa. "Were they as angry as they looked last night?"

Lisa slumped against the wall beside Carole. "Oh,

no," she said. "When you saw them last night, they were still being polite. They were *much* angrier than they looked."

Because all the girls were supposed to have been spending the night at Lisa's, one of the first things Mr. and Mrs. Lake had done, after helping Carole out of the pool, was to call Lisa's parents. Needless to say, Mr. and Mrs. Atwood were not delighted to have their bridge game interrupted by the call. They had come to get Lisa and Carole, whose overnight bags were still at Lisa's house. Colonel Hanson had picked Carole up from Lisa's house within half an hour. The sleepover had been over without anyone's having slept at all.

"No, my parents weren't very happy," Lisa repeated. She picked up a twig and used it to draw a design in the dirt. "Apparently covering the neighbor's lawn with toilet paper is not what my mother considers ladylike behavior. Neither is sneaking out of the house and then using a ladder to spy on other people."

"Chad's not other people," Carole said. "He's Stevie's brother."

"I know, but my mother wasn't in the mood to see the difference."

Carole nodded sympathetically. She had to admit, once the Lakes had turned on all the outside lights by the pool, the crime scene had looked pretty disastrous.

Most of Mrs. Lake's flowers were not going to survive, and Carole had her doubts about the tomato plants.

"The strange thing is, I have a brother," Lisa continued. "But he's so much older than me, I hardly know him. I mean, I don't know him well enough to fight with him. In a way that's kind of sad. My mother seems to think that most families are like ours—she doesn't understand why Stevie would fight with her brothers at all. She said our actions were 'totally uncalled for.' Her words exactly."

"I think my father thought it was funny," Carole said. "I mean, he'd never say so, but he gets this little look in the back of his eyes."

"So you're not in trouble, really?"

"Oh, no, I'm in plenty of trouble, really." Carole sighed. Just because her father was amused didn't mean he was going to let her get away with anything. "I'm on KP for the next month."

"What's KP?"

"Kitchen Police. I have to cook, and wash all the dishes." Carole looked up at Lisa and grinned. "Still, I suppose it could be worse."

Lisa shook her head. "Not for Stevie."

Carole's grin vanished instantly. "You're right," she said.

"The worst part," Lisa continued, "was that it was our

24

fault just as much as hers, but she's getting most of the blame. We went along with her. We thought the whole thing was funny. And you know the TP'ing was my idea." The thought weighed heavily on Lisa's conscience. She was supposed to be the well-behaved one. For once she had led Stevie astray, not the other way around, and now Stevie was paying for it.

"If you hadn't thought of TP'ing, Stevie or I would have thought of something just as bad," Carole said comfortingly. "We were all to blame." She yawned.

"Are you sleepy?" Lisa asked.

"Sure."

"Me too. Getting up at seven A.M. to take toilet paper off bushes isn't exactly my idea of fun."

They had spent two hours at the Lakes' that morning, cleaning the front lawn. Stevie's idea of watering all the TP didn't seem so inspired when they were the ones picking off each individual shred from each individual leaf from each individual tree and bush in the yard. Stevie had helped them, but she had been absolutely forbidden to speak to either of them—and since Mrs. Lake had sat on the front porch the entire time, reading the Sunday paper and supervising them, Stevie hadn't tried.

All three members of The Saddle Club were going to have to share the cost of replacing the torn screen door and the trampled flowers. Stevie was going to have to replant the flowers. None of that seemed too bad—in fact, it seemed fair.

"But camp!" Carole groaned suddenly. "How can they do that to Stevie! When she's hardly ridden all summer!"

"I know," Lisa said. "I can't believe her parents would be so cruel."

Stephanie Lake had been absolutely, positively, and completely grounded for the next two weeks. She was not allowed out of the house, except to replant the flowers. She was not allowed to go even once to Pine Hollow. She was not allowed to speak to the rest of The Saddle Club—she couldn't even phone them.

She was not allowed to go to camp.

Carole felt her heart twist. This was the worst of all possible punishments. Carole would gladly have done KP for years if it meant Stevie could go to camp. She would have listened to her father's lecture on responsible behavior thirteen million times.

"My mother sat me down for a little talk this morning," Lisa said. "She said she doesn't know what to do with me, but she's going to start by having me perform community service. Her women's auxiliary has a vegetable garden, and they send all the produce to the county homeless shelter. I've been made the chief weed-picker."

She sighed. "I'd pick all the weeds in Willow Creek if it meant Stevie could go to camp with us."

In the pasture Delilah, a palomino mare, suddenly squealed and bucked. She ran down to the far corner and galloped back. It looked like pure good spirits to Carole—the mare was having fun. Carole wished she felt like that. She wondered if she ever would again.

"It's so totally unfair," she said to Lisa. "When you consider how little time Stevie's gotten to spend on horseback this summer—or with Phil . . ." Carole's voice trailed off. She'd never had a real boyfriend, so she didn't really know what it would feel like to be separated from one. But she could well imagine what it would feel like not to ride. "If I couldn't see Starlight for two whole weeks, I would just die."

"The worst part," Lisa said bitterly, "is how that brat Chad got away totally scot-free." It was true. In all the commotion, Stevie's parents had never noticed Chad making faces out his window, and by the time they'd gotten back inside, Stevie's riding boots had been sitting in their usual place in her bedroom closet, buried under her dirty breeches just the way she'd left them. Chad had put them back, of course, but he claimed he'd never touched them.

Carole and Lisa knew that Chad, not Stevie, was lying. Unfortunately, Stevie's parents didn't.

"We've got to find a way to make Stevie's parents change their minds," Lisa said. "We've just got to. Camp won't be any fun without her."

"We need to get even with Chad, too," Carole said. "We can't let him get away with this."

Lisa looked at Carole. She smiled for what felt like the first time in days. "We need to out-Stevie Stevie," she said. "What we need here is a Stevie plan."

AFTER WATCHING THE HORSES graze for a few more minutes, Lisa and Carole went back into the stable. They stopped outside Belle's stall.

"Poor Belle," Carole said, patting the mare's soft nose. "We should groom her, since Stevie can't." They took Belle out of her stall and brushed her until her coat gleamed. Lisa carefully combed her mane and tail. When they were finished, Carole put the grooming bucket away. Lisa took a piece of paper out of her pocket. It was a sign reading PLEASE TAKE GOOD CARE OF MY HORSE WHILE I'M GROUNDED. Stevie had handed it to Lisa that morning.

Carole came back just as Lisa was taping the sign to the front of Belle's stall. "I told Max about Stevie," she said. "He said he'd make sure Belle got turned out regularly. I told him we'd handle the grooming."

"I think we should keep the sign up anyway," Lisa said. "That way Red will know, too. I haven't seen him yet today." Red O'Malley was Pine Hollow's stable hand.

Carole nodded glumly. "Well," she said with a sigh, "should we go on a trail ride?"

"I guess so," Lisa said. Even though she loved trail rides, she didn't feel very enthusiastic about going on one today. Trail rides weren't the same without Stevie.

Even out in the beautiful green woods, Lisa's spirits failed to lift. When she wasn't thinking about the disaster of the night before, and the horror of Stevie's not being with them at camp, she found herself thinking about her failure in the lesson the day before. If only she'd been able to get Barq to lengthen his stride! Lisa was still upset about her shortcomings as a rider. Today she was riding Prancer again. She thought about asking Prancer to lengthen on the trail, but she wasn't sure it would make her feel better even if Prancer lengthened perfectly.

In the first place, Lisa knew that Prancer did the movement much more easily than Barq. In the second place, Lisa wasn't sure it was fair to ask the mare to work hard when they were supposed to be having fun on the trail. And in the third place—Lisa reluctantly admitted to herself—she didn't want to try the exercise in front of Carole. Carole would know right away what Lisa was doing, and why, and no doubt she'd know exactly what Lisa's problem was, too, and be able to tell her how to fix it. Lisa didn't want to be faced with further evidence that Carole was a better rider.

Plus, what if Lisa tried to do it in front of Carole and failed entirely? That would be the worst thing. Carole rode so well. Lisa shuddered and tried to think of something else. But the only something else her mind seemed interested in was Stevie. Camp without Stevie. Lisa sighed. She'd never felt so depressed while sitting on a horse.

Carole heard Lisa sigh and knew exactly how she felt. Even though riding Starlight was always a joy, without Stevie the trail ride wasn't the same. "Without Stevie, camp won't be the same, either," Carole said.

"I know," Lisa said. "It kind of amazes me how this all happened. Not Stevie's being grounded—I understand how that happened. I mean how it all got started—how she fights with her brothers all the time. Especially Chad. Do you understand it?"

"Do I understand sibling rivalry, you mean?" Carole

asked with a laugh. "Think about it, Lisa. I'm the only one of us who doesn't have any siblings. How could I?" She smoothed Starlight's mane.

"I've got a sibling, but I don't think we have a typical sibling relationship," Lisa replied. "Most of the kids at school seem to fight with their brothers and sisters a lot. I never fought with mine when he still lived at home."

Carole nodded. Suddenly she remembered how she had felt when her father's girlfriend's daughter, Marie, had stayed with them. Carole's father had paid a lot of attention to Marie, and at first it had made Carole jealous. "Jealousy," Carole said. "That's part of it."

"You think Stevie and Chad are jealous of each other?" Lisa asked. "I don't know. I think they just like playing tricks on each other."

Carole had to admit that Stevie never really seemed to want what Chad had, or vice versa. "Well, okay," she said, "but even if I don't understand sibling rivalry entirely, I think I'm starting to get the idea." She grinned. "In fact, I'm starting to feel just like Stevie feels. Now *I* want to get even with Chad. It's his fault Stevie's missing camp!" She shook her head. "Let's canter!"

Lisa gladly agreed. They let their horses canter along the edge of a meadow grown tall with flowering grasses. A bird flew out of the grass, startling Starlight. Carole steadied him with a quiet murmur and a soft hand. Starlight quickly regained his composure. Lisa felt another pang of envy at this latest example of Carole's beautiful riding.

The girls brought their horses back to a trot as they entered the woods.

"We have to find a way for Stevie to go to camp," Lisa said.

"I agree," Carole said. "We've got to spring her somehow. I just don't know how."

They discussed the problem for several minutes. "What if we apologize?" Lisa suggested at last. "What if we tell Mr. and Mrs. Lake that everything was our idea, and our fault and only our fault? If they think Stevie didn't have anything to do with it, maybe they'll unground her."

"Maybe," Carole said after a moment's thought. "I doubt it, but after all, Stevie's parents can't ground us."

"Right," said Lisa. "There's no risk. We just have to grovel."

"For Stevie's sake, I can grovel a lot," Carole said firmly. "The only problem is that apologizing doesn't help us get even with Chad. But we can deal with him later."

* * *

THEY RETURNED TO Pine Hollow, took care of their horses, and walked over to the Lakes' house.

"Okay," Lisa said as she rang the doorbell, "get ready to grovel."

Carole laughed nervously. "You're the actress." Lisa had once played the lead role in *Annie* with the Willow Creek Community Theater.

"Carole," Lisa said gently, "this isn't hard. Remember, they can't ground us." Lisa had always thought Stevie's parents were nice, especially considering all they had to put up with from Stevie and her brothers.

"You're just better at this stuff than I am," Carole said. Before Lisa could reply, the door opened. Chad was standing there. He was wearing his soccer uniform and no shoes.

"Sorry," he said, closing the door partway, "Stevie's in solitary. No visitors. No phone calls. Bread and water twice a day." He grinned wickedly.

Carole put her foot in the door. "You creep! I suppose you think it's funny that—"

"Chad," Lisa cut in softly, "Carole and I want to talk to your parents, not Stevie. Are they home?"

"Sure." Chad shrugged. He let them inside and pointed down the hall to the back door—the one with the ripped screen. Carole winced. It hadn't been repaired yet. "They're by the pool. Help yourself." He walked into the living room, turned the television up a little louder, and began dribbling a soccer ball around the room.

"Creep," Carole repeated under her breath. "I'm glad I don't have a brother!"

Lisa grinned. It wasn't like Carole to be this upset. But Lisa knew how devastated Carole would be if she had to miss camp. Carole was just feeling devastated on Stevie's behalf.

Lisa was upset, too, but suddenly she felt confident. The Saddle Club had never failed. They wouldn't fail now. They wouldn't let Stevie miss camp.

"WELL," LISA SAID as she and Carole walked out the front door, "I would have groveled on my hands and knees, but I'm not sure even that would have helped."

"No," Carole said. "I don't think it would have. They didn't budge an inch."

Lisa shook her head. She had been as polite and earnest as she knew how, but Stevie's parents hadn't believed for a second that Stevie was blameless. Even if she had been, Mrs. Lake had said, that was not the point.

"I didn't know Stevie had done all that other stuff, did you?" Lisa asked.

Carole shook her head. "I knew about Chad's clothes, of course, but I didn't know about the tacks in his soccer shoes. Or that Stevie let all the air out of his soccer ball and bicycle tires and then hid the air pump. She didn't tell us about that."

"Chad can't prove Stevie did it. It could have been Alex, or even Michael."

"That's what Mr. Lake said."

"Yeah." Lisa sighed. "He also said it didn't matter." That was the crux of the problem. Stevie's parents weren't interested in proof. They were pretty sure Stevie was behind most of the pranks they knew about, and they were pretty sure she was behind other pranks they didn't know about, and they were tired of living in a combat zone. Stevie was grounded. Two weeks, no early parole. No way.

"Nice try, girls," Mr. Lake had said to Carole and Lisa.

"Oh well," Lisa said. They ducked around the side of Stevie's yard to take the shortcut back to Pine Hollow. Stevie's bedroom window was two stories above them, and they paused to look up at their friend. Sure enough, Stevie was sitting by the window, looking sadly in the direction of Pine Hollow. Lisa knew that from Stevie's room you could just see the top of the weathervane on the stable roof.

When Stevie saw them, she waved frantically. Carole and Lisa waved back. Stevie held up one finger and then disappeared.

"She wants us to wait," Carole said.

"I hope she doesn't try to climb down on a bedsheet or something," Lisa said. "If she gets in trouble again, she'll be grounded for life."

In a moment Stevie was back. She opened her window and sailed a tiny paper airplane down to her friends. Lisa caught it and unfolded it. Stevie had written them a note.

I heard you talking to my parents, it read. *Thanks for trying. I can't talk—I promised I wouldn't.* Lisa smiled. No matter what, Stevie never broke promises. That was why she so rarely made them. *But they never said I couldn't write notes. How's Belle?*

Lisa tried to pantomime *She's fine*. She didn't do it very well. Stevie looked puzzled. Lisa wished she knew sign language.

"*We* can talk," Carole said to Lisa. "And I think Stevie's allowed to listen."

Stevie nodded, grinning. Lisa smiled. "Of course. Stevie, Belle's fine."

"We hung your sign, and we groomed her for you," Carole added.

"And don't worry about camp," Lisa said firmly. "We're going to spring you. We made it a Saddle Club project."

Stevie gave them a thumbs-up sign.

"We've got a plan," Lisa added. "Don't worry. It'll work for sure."

5

" 'WE'VE GOT A PLAN'?" Carole repeated as they hit the main road back to Pine Hollow. "We don't have a plan! Or if we do, I don't know about it!"

"I know," Lisa said. "We don't have one."

"Then why did you tell Stevie we did?"

"We'll get one," Lisa replied. Even though groveling to Stevie's parents hadn't helped, Lisa still felt confident. "Besides," she continued, "I didn't want Stevie to feel desperate. If she feels desperate, she'll come up with a plan of her own, and who knows what'll happen then."

Carole shuddered. Usually it was Stevie who came up

with their plans, and usually what she came up with was good, but if Stevie got caught doing something else wrong now, she'd be grounded until her hair turned gray. Carole saw Lisa's point.

Back at Pine Hollow, they sat on the hay bales outside Belle's stall and tried hard to think of some way to help Stevie. Lisa remembered Mr. and Mrs. Lake's polite, unyielding faces. This wasn't going to be easy.

"What's wrong, girls? Why the long faces? You look like somebody got your goat. And where's Stevie?" It was Mrs. Reg, Max Regnery's mother. She ran the stable. She had come to get one of the bales they were sitting on.

"Oh, Mrs. Reg, didn't Max tell you?" Carole asked. She and Lisa helped Mrs. Reg break the hay bale apart and feed it to the horses nearby. While they worked, they told her the whole story.

"I see," Mrs. Reg said, nodding. "That's too bad."

"Stevie and Chad have been fighting all summer," Lisa added. "Stevie did some things she shouldn't, but Chad did, too, and he isn't being punished at all."

Mrs. Reg nodded again sympathetically. "You know," she said, "I don't know if I ever told you, but the expression 'get your goat' is actually a horse term."

Carole and Lisa exchanged agonized glances. Mrs. Reg was famous for her stories, which usually seemed pointless, though they often weren't. But now? Talking about goats when they were so worried about Stevie?

"Yes," Mrs. Reg continued, not seeming to notice how the girls squirmed, "it comes from racing. Many horses, you know, feel uncomfortable in strange environments, and a racehorse that isn't happy won't do well on the track. At the same time, racehorses are always being moved to different racetracks and different stalls. So, especially in the old days but sometimes even now, racehorses often traveled with an animal companion, such as a goat. The horse felt comfortable with his goat friend around, even when everything else was different."

Carole suppressed a sigh. She'd heard all this before. Mrs. Reg went on. "So, if you wanted to upset someone else's racehorse, you stole his goat. You got his goat!" Mrs. Reg smiled.

"We know that story, Mrs. Reg," Lisa said politely. "When we went to the Preakness with Max and Deborah, some of the horses there had goats." Lisa was surprised that Mrs. Reg didn't remember this. She rarely forgot anything.

Mrs. Reg nodded and patted Lisa's arm. "It's always good to consider all your resources," she said gently. She paused to pat Belle, too. "Poor mare," Mrs. Reg said sadly. "Poor, lonely Belle." The office telephone rang, and Mrs. Reg hurried away.

"What was that about?" Carole asked in amazement. "The goat story again? And why was she so sorry for Belle? She should be sorry for Stevie!" Really, Carole couldn't remember a time when Mrs. Reg had been so vague—and that was saying something.

Lisa scrunched down on the remaining hay bale, thinking hard. She was sure there had to be some meaning in what Mrs. Reg said. Suddenly she jumped up. "I've got it!" she said. She hugged Carole. "That's it! The plan!"

Carole cheered. "Tell me all about it!"

A FEW MINUTES LATER they knocked on the door of Max's office. Mrs. Reg wasn't there anymore, but Max was sitting at his desk, looking at the lesson schedule.

"Well," he said when he saw them. "How are you two holding up?"

"Pretty well, considering everything," Lisa said.

"Considering that we got up at seven to clean toilet paper off bushes," Carole added.

Max grinned. "If I remember right, taking the toilet paper off the bushes is never as much fun as putting it on."

Lisa couldn't imagine Max TP'ing anybody. "We've got a favor to ask you," she said. "We just remembered that Stevie wanted Belle to have her teeth fixed—"

42

"Floated," Carole corrected.

Lisa winced. She still didn't know the right words. When would she learn?

"Sure," Max said, nodding. "It's been almost a year since she had Belle's teeth done, hasn't it?"

"Yeah," Carole said, "and Belle's starting to act as if bridling hurts her."

"So would you mind calling Judy Barker for Stevie?" Lisa asked. "Because Stevie's not allowed to use the phone."

"No problem," Max assured them. "It's a good time to have it done, since Stevie won't be riding for a few weeks. I'll have Judy come out as soon as she can."

"And then"—Lisa paused—"do you think you could call Stevie's parents and tell them when the appointment is, so Stevie knows about it? We'd call them, but . . . Stevie's parents aren't exactly happy with us right now." She looked down at her feet. Carole gave a sad sigh.

Max chuckled. "I'll bet not," he said. "Don't worry about it. I'll take care of everything."

"Thanks, Max!" They left the office.

"THAT WENT WELL," Carole said as they walked out of the stable and headed down the road toward the Willow Creek shopping center.

43

"Yep," Lisa said briskly. "The first step is in place. Now it's time for some research!" She felt energized, much better than she had felt that morning, or, really, anytime since their lesson the day before. "Good thing I got my allowance yesterday morning—before you guys spent the night!"

"You mean before we spent half the night," Carole said.

"Yeah," Lisa said. "Even after paying for the screen door, I've got something left. But if we'd gotten in trouble first, I bet my parents would have kept my allowance, too. See—we were lucky about something, after all!"

Carole smiled. Lisa's enthusiasm was contagious. Carole felt much better, too. She thought it was just possible that Lisa's plan might work.

THEY RETURNED ONCE AGAIN to the stable, this time armed with several small bags from various fast-food restaurants. They took them all into Belle's stall. Carole checked the aisle. "No Max," she reported. "No Red, no Mrs. Reg, no nobody. We're all clear." There were no lessons on Sunday, and the stables were usually quiet.

"Good." Lisa rummaged through the bags and pulled out a paper cup. "Number one. Diet Coke." She held it under Belle's nose.

Belle sniffed the rim of the cup curiously.

"I don't think she likes it," Lisa said.

"Give her time," Carole said cautiously. "Let her get used to it."

Lisa knew Carole was right. They couldn't afford to have this part of their plan fail.

Belle stuck the tip of her nose into the cup. She slurped once, then drew back, startled. "I don't think she likes the fizz," Carole said. She took the cup from Lisa, used a straw to stir some of the fizz out of the soda, and offered it to Belle again. This time the mare took a cautious sip, then another.

"Oh no," Lisa groaned. "She likes it."

Carole laughed. "Who'd have guessed?"

They set the diet Coke out of the way and opened the second bag. "Orange juice," said Lisa.

The orange juice didn't work out, either—Belle actually drank the whole cup! She also seemed partial to the sweetened iced tea they gave her—she didn't drink all of it, but almost.

"She's got a sweet tooth," Lisa said.

"Just like Stevie. Try the milk."

Belle, now eager for more treats, nosed the carton expectantly and, when Lisa opened it wide enough, plunged her nose into it. She drew back, looking appalled, and tried to shake the milk off the end of her nose.

45

"Yeah!" Lisa said. "She doesn't like it! That's it!" She began to gather up the used bags.

"We've got to be sure," Carole said. "She doesn't like it by itself, but that may not mean much." Carole went to the feed room while Lisa waited impatiently. Sure enough, even though Belle refused to drink the milk alone, she was more than willing to eat a handful of grain soaked in it.

Lisa tried not to feel annoyed because Carole was right again. "We've got one more," she said. "If this doesn't work, we'll have to go back to the shopping center." She pulled out the cup of lukewarm black coffee she'd saved for last. "Here goes." She stuck it under Belle's nose.

Belle seemed offended by the very smell of the coffee. She backed away from the cup, refusing to take a single sip. Carole put a handful of grain in her feed bucket, and Lisa poured some of the coffee over it. Belle sniffed the grain, then ignored it.

"Bingo!" said Lisa. She gave Carole a high five. They gathered all the cups and bags together.

Carole watched Belle closely. "I don't think she'll eat that at all right now," she said. "But remember, she just had her lunch. If she's really hungry, a little coffee might not be enough to stop her."

Lisa nodded. As usual, Carole was making sense. "It'll all depend on timing," she said.

"Poor Belle," Carole added. She scooped the doctored grain into one of the paper bags and gave the mare a pat.

"Belle's fine," Lisa said. She paused, thinking about the details of her plan. "What we need now," she declared, "is some nice, fine dirt."

Carole laughed. "Whatever you say."

6

EARLY THE NEXT MORNING Carole and Lisa knocked on the door of Stevie's house.

"Do you think this will work?" Carole asked Lisa.

"Shhh," Lisa said.

The door opened. It was Chad again. "What do you want?" he asked. "Stevie's still in solitary. I can't let you see her." He was wearing the same soccer jersey he'd had on the day before, but this time he was also wearing socks and one soccer shoe and carrying the other shoe.

Lisa made her voice solemn and sad. "We need to talk to your parents again," she said. "It's important."

"They aren't here," he said with a puzzled frown. "You know that. They're at work." Lisa did indeed know that. Fortunately, she knew the schedule at the Lake household very well. She and Carole exchanged glances.

"Well," Carole said with a little shrug, "I guess we'll have to tell Davey, then." Davey was the college student hired to look after Stevie and her brothers for the summer.

Chad put on his second shoe and began tying the laces. "You can't do that, either. He took Alex and Michael to their baseball practices." Chad stood up. "You'll have to come back, if it's important."

Lisa sat down on one of the chairs in the living room. "If we can't tell your parents or Davey, we'll have to tell you," she said firmly. "It's very important. We can't waste time."

Carole followed Lisa's lead and sat down on the couch. Chad watched them, clearly irritated by the way they made themselves at home. Lisa patted the seat of the chair next to hers. "Sit down," she said. "We're sorry to bring bad news."

Chad sat, looking wary.

"It's very serious," Carole said in funereal tones. "Belle's sick."

When Carole had said it was serious, Chad had started to look concerned. When she said the trouble was Belle, however, he laughed. "What happened?" he asked. "Did she bonk her head like Stevie did? That'd be pretty funny!" Then, seeing the looks the two girls gave him, Chad wiped the smile off his face. "Sorry. Guess you wouldn't think that was funny, huh?"

"Guess not," Carole said. Oh, she couldn't stand brothers! Laughing about a horse being sick! Not for the first time, Carole was grateful she was an only child.

"So," Chad said, "what's wrong? Does she have the sniffles? She didn't break a leg, did she?" He looked ready to laugh again. Carole looked ready to throttle him.

Lisa intervened quickly. "Belle's pining," she said. "Horses are such sensitive creatures. They don't adjust well to change. Belle's not eating."

"We think she's missing Stevie," Carole said, shooting Chad a dirty look. *And it's all your fault,* she thought but didn't say. Then she remembered that Belle wasn't really missing Stevie. She shouldn't blame Chad for things that hadn't actually happened. "She's just not herself," Carole continued in a softer tone.

"Horses have very delicate digestive systems," Lisa went on. "Any little thing can throw them off. And any sort of digestive trouble—well . . ." She let her voice fade away and looked to Carole for support.

". . . it can be very serious," Carole said.

50

"Very," Lisa whispered.

"Oh, come off it," Chad said. "Give me a break, will you?" He picked up his soccer ball and bounced it a few times. "You expect me to believe that Stevie's horse is sick because it misses her? I've been around horses, too, you know, and they aren't that smart. Plus, Belle weighs, like, a thousand pounds. She could not eat for a month and be okay." He looked sideways at Lisa. "You guys made this up, right? Did Stevie put you up to it?"

With difficulty Lisa maintained her earnest, sorrowful expression. "I wish we were joking," she said. "I wish this were just another prank. But it's not."

"It's been building for a long time," Carole added. She looked at her fingernails, because she knew that if she looked at Chad she'd want to hurt him. "Since her accident, Stevie hasn't been able to spend much time with Belle. Horses are herd animals, you know. They rely on their companions."

"And Stevie, of course, is Belle's main herd," Lisa said. "In Belle's mind, Stevie is like another horse." Lisa didn't dare look at Carole. They'd both start laughing. Lisa tried to remember the public television show she'd seen on zebras. "You see, horses establish patterns of domination in the herd. Lower-caste members look to the alpha members for guidance and direction. Without Stevie, Belle feels rudderless, like a ship lost at sea." Lisa

51

let her voice tremble. She saw Carole's knee twitch slightly in response to that last ridiculous statement. She brushed her hand across her eyes, as if to wipe away a tear.

"Horses are big, strong animals," Carole cut in quickly. She had to say something before Lisa came up with some other declaration about rudderless ships. "But sometimes they can be affected by very minor things. Horses can die from eating too much grain. They can also die from eating too little. A normal horse eats twenty-five pounds of food a day, so if the horse suddenly eats nothing, it's a big change."

"Physiologically," Lisa added, "horses are designed to graze continuously." Carole's knee twitched again.

Chad's face had grown more concerned. He quit bouncing his ball. "You're not kidding, are you? You're really worried."

"Well, of course we're worried!" Carole snapped. "Stevie's our best friend!" *We're worried that Stevie won't go to camp,* Carole thought. *We're very worried about that.*

"Max is aware of Belle's condition," Lisa said. "He's pretty concerned, so he might call the vet, Judy Barker."

"Good," Chad said, nodding. "That's a great idea. The vet'll fix Belle."

"Well . . . ," Lisa said. She looked sadly at Carole, who shrugged gloomily.

"I'm sure Judy will try," Carole said. "But if the problem really is that Belle is pining, that she's not getting enough attention and that she's really missing Stevie, there's not much Judy can do."

"Modern medicine can only go so far," Lisa intoned. Carole bit her lips to keep from giggling.

"But Stevie's only grounded for two weeks," Chad said. "I mean," he added jokingly, "it's not that long. Belle'll survive." He grinned at Lisa and Carole. His grin faded when they didn't grin back.

"We hope she will," Carole said softly. "Only . . . any kind of digestive disturbance in a horse can lead to colic, you know. And colic . . ." She let her voice trail off.

"Colic can be fatal," Lisa said. "Horses die of it all the time."

"Seriously?" Chad asked. "Do you seriously know any horses that have died of colitch?"

"Colic," Carole corrected him. "Yes, I seriously do. Two." This, Carole reflected, of all the things she had said, was entirely true. Fortunately no horses at Pine Hollow had colicked badly in the past few years, but Carole had ridden at a lot of stables around the country during the traveling part of her father's military career. She'd known a lot of horses.

Lisa shivered at the unmistakable ring of truth in Carole's voice. What if Belle really did get sick! For a moment Lisa almost believed her own story.

"Gosh," Chad said, "I never knew anything like this could happen."

"Well," Lisa said, "that's understandable. You really haven't spent that much time around horses." Chad was the only one of Stevie's brothers who had ever ridden at all. Lisa blushed slightly at the memory. Chad had taken lessons for a few weeks because—well, because he'd wanted to get to know Lisa better. They'd gone to a movie together, only to discover that their tastes in most things were very different.

Including our taste in practical jokes, Lisa thought. *No bucket of water over the door for me. This sort of revenge is much more my style.* She could tell that Chad was starting to believe everything they'd said.

"Please, whatever you do, don't tell Stevie about this," Lisa said. "We don't want her worrying."

"Please," Carole added. "She'd worry a lot." They both knew that if Stevie heard a word about anything's being seriously wrong with Belle, she'd break the sound barrier getting over to Pine Hollow, grounded or not.

"Just tell your parents, please, that Max might call," Lisa said. "Don't let them worry too much, either. Carole and I will let you know how Belle is doing. We'll give her as much attention as we can."

54

"Don't tell Stevie," Carole repeated. "After all, there's nothing she can do anyway. She can't leave the house for two weeks."

"Right," said Chad. "Okay."

"Thanks, Chad," Lisa said. "We knew we could count on you." She smiled sadly at him. She thought about shaking his hand or something, but feared it would be too much. She got up from her chair, and Carole followed. Chad went with them to the door.

"I'm sorry about Stevie's horse," he said.

"So are we," Carole said. "We'll let you know how she's doing."

"Thanks," Chad said uncertainly. He closed the door, and the girls heard his soccer ball bounce just once and then stop.

"Let's get out of sight before we explode!" Lisa hissed. She and Carole dashed around the corner of the house, crouched under the bushes, and laughed until their sides hurt. Until she'd started laughing, Lisa hadn't realized how tense she was. The conversation with Chad had been nerve-racking. So much depended on his believing them right from the start.

"Explain to me again," Carole said, gasping for breath, "how Belle is like a—a—rudderless ship—lost—at sea!" She whooped with laughter.

"And, you know, Stevie is Belle's main herd!" Lisa

laughed so much she could hardly breathe. She tried to keep it quiet. What if Chad could hear them from inside the house? "We've got to get out of here," she said.

"Let's say hi to Stevie first," Carole suggested. They got up and went to Stevie's window. This time she wasn't in view, and Lisa had to throw sticks at the window to get her attention. When she saw them, Stevie immediately opened her window and waved. Soon a paper airplane floated down.

Hi! it read. *I'm so bored! I hate Chad! Have you read* National Velvet? *What's new?*

"Nothing's new," Carole said. "We're bored without you, too. Of course we've read *National Velvet*. We just wanted to say hi."

"We *really* detest Chad," Lisa added. "Does Chad ever change out of his soccer clothes?"

Stevie shrugged. She pinched her nose between her fingers and made a face as if she were smelling Chad's old socks. Lisa and Carole laughed.

After a few minutes of one-sided conversation, they said good-bye and left. As they were walking back to Pine Hollow, Lisa asked Carole, "Don't you think we should tell Stevie? Wouldn't it be better if she knew?"

Carole shook her head. "The only way we could tell her is if we shout up to her window. We can't take the chance that Chad would hear us. If he did, it would totally wreck our plan."

"You're right. We can't chance it," said Lisa. "Stevie *has* to go to camp. And Chad *has* to suffer!"

"Suffer he will," said Carole, her dark eyes glinting mischievously. "Suffer he will!"

LISA OPENED THE DOOR of the stable office. "Max," she asked, "would it be okay if I took Barq out and worked with him in the outdoor ring?"

Max looked up from the lunch he was eating at his desk with his wife, Deborah. "Sure," he said with a smile. "I don't need the ring again until two o'clock, and Barq's only been in a beginner lesson so far today. But you can take Prancer if you want to. She's not being worked much today, either."

"Thanks, Max." Lisa shifted her weight from foot to foot. "I think—I think I'd rather ride Barq today."

"That's fine." As Lisa turned to leave, Max added, "I think there are a few stalls that still need cleaning. Red left for his summer-school class. Maybe after you ride—"

"I'll do them, Max! Don't worry!" This was one of the nicest things about Pine Hollow, Lisa thought as she went to get Barq's saddle. Max expected everyone to help with the chores, but in return he was very generous about letting his students ride even when they weren't taking lessons. It was a great deal.

Lisa patted Barq as she went into his stall. "We're going to do it right today," she told him. Carole had had to go to the doctor's for her camp physical, so Lisa knew she would have a little time to work entirely alone, and entirely alone was how she wanted it. She and Barq were going to work on lengthening his stride, all by themselves, without advice from friends who knew everything. This was one time Lisa wanted to learn something on her own.

She groomed Barq, tacked him up, and led him into the outdoor arena. Some of the pole grids from Saturday's lesson were still in place, and Lisa quickly reassembled the others. She moved some of the poles to normal trot length and others to extended trot. She didn't keep any of them at short trot length, because she knew Barq was already good at that.

As she mounted, Lisa gave herself a little pep talk.

She had handled Chad well this morning. She had come up with a plan. *Surely,* she thought, *I can get one stubborn Arabian horse to lengthen his trot.* She began by trotting and cantering Barq around the ring several times, to warm him up and loosen his muscles.

After several minutes she brought him back to a trot and started working through the pole grids. The normal trot grid was no problem. Barq skillfully put his feet down in the spaces between the poles. Lisa sucked in her breath and aimed him at a longer grid. Barq started correctly, but his too-short stride made his feet whack the poles. *Whack, whack, whack.* Lisa sighed. Just like their lesson!

She circled the arena again. *Whack, whack, whack.* She tried coming from the other direction. *Clank, clank, clank.* She concentrated fiercely, trying hard to remember every single thing Max had told her. Heels down, legs tight against Barq's sides, urging him forward with every stride. Hands low, steady, giving, to encourage the horse to stretch himself forward. Chest up, shoulders square, eyes straight ahead.

Whack, whack, whack. She felt like whacking Barq. She knew, however, that almost all mistakes were the rider's fault, not the horse's—it was the rider's job to tell the horse what to do and get the horse to cooperate.

Barq did not seem especially cooperative today. Lisa

wondered what she was doing wrong. Whenever she used her legs to push him forward, he speeded up instead of taking longer strides, and when she used her hands to slow him back down, he set his jaw against her. Lisa breathed deeply. She would get this right. She would.

Whack, whack, whack. *"Arrghhh!"* Lisa shouted in annoyance.

"I think one of the problems is that you're giving with your hands too much, and too soon," Carole said quietly. Lisa jumped and turned in the saddle. Carole was leaning against the side of the fence, watching. Lisa hadn't even known she was there.

Lisa was already frustrated, and now being startled by Carole was too much.

"Oh, of course you would know what my problem is!" Lisa shouted. "You know everything about horses! You've even got one! You and Stevie both have horses, and I don't, and it's not fair!"

For a moment the friends stared at each other. Lisa blinked. She never lost her temper like that, especially not at Carole, and she was instantly sorry. At the same time she still felt full of boiling anger and a sense of injustice.

"I know it's not fair," Carole answered. She looked at Lisa with concern. "Stevie and I really wish you had a horse, too."

The bubble of anger inside Lisa burst at this quiet declaration of sympathy. For a moment she thought she might cry. "I'm sorry," she said. "I shouldn't yell at you. None of this is your fault. And I know I should be glad that I at least get to ride—I mean, Max lets me ride almost whenever I want—but I always know less than you and Stevie, and I'm always having to catch up. Both of you could do this, even on Barq. I can't."

Carole nodded. "I bet it is hard," she said. "Stevie and I have been riding for so much longer than you. But, Lisa, you know an awful lot, and Max always talks about what a fast learner you are."

"I didn't know about teeth filing," Lisa retorted. "I mean, teeth *floating*. I've never known any horses that died of colic. And I can't get Barq to lengthen."

Carole looked thoughtful. "Be glad you never saw a horse die of colic," she said. Then she smiled. "Maybe you didn't know about teeth or colic," she added, "but you can say things like 'physically, horses are designed to graze continuously' without even pausing to think about it. I could never do that!"

Lisa had to smile in return. "It's *physiologically*, not *physically*," she said. "It doesn't mean quite the same thing."

Carole grinned. "See? That's exactly what I mean." She looked at Barq. "And you will get him to lengthen,

Lisa; it just might take a little more work. Would you like me to help you, or would you rather I just went away?"

Lisa thought about how glad she was to have a friend like Carole, who understood her so well. She felt a little better now that she'd talked about what was bothering her. "I guess I'd like your help," she said. "If you wouldn't mind."

Carole opened the gate and came into the arena. "I never mind, you know that. But I probably sound bossy sometimes. I don't mean to, but if I ever start to annoy you, let me know, okay?"

"Okay."

Carole replaced some of the poles that Barq had whacked out of position. Lisa picked up a trot again.

"Now," Carole said as Lisa turned the corner before the poles, "use your leg but keep your hand steady. Then give with your hand as he starts to move into it. Give a lot, but not too much."

"That's useful," Lisa said with a laugh. "When does it start to be too much?"

"When he speeds up," Carole said. "That's it! Good!"

Barq dropped his head, and for a moment Lisa thought he was getting it. They flowed over the poles, one-two-three-four-*whack*. Barq's hooves hit the very last one.

"Yuck," said Lisa.

"Much better," Carole praised her. "Could you feel the difference?"

"I think so," Lisa said, but she wasn't sure. She tried several more times, but she never quite got it. Sometimes Barq would start to lengthen, but Lisa couldn't get him to maintain his gait. He always whacked the last pole or two on the grid.

After they'd tried another half dozen times, Lisa pulled him to a halt. "That's enough," she said, giving Barq a pat. "I wish we'd done better, but I'm just going to upset him if we keep going. He's doing his best. It's me who's not getting it."

Carole also wished that Lisa had gotten it right. She rarely saw her friend so upset about her riding, and she sympathized. She wished Lisa had a horse.

Carole also thought Lisa was doing the right thing to stop before Barq became tired and cross. "You made good progress," she said encouragingly. "He'll get it next time."

Lisa rolled her eyes. "Maybe. Want to go on a trail ride? I'll walk Barq around out here while you get Starlight." Carole readily agreed and hurried into the stable. Lisa watched her go with a strange mixture of affection and irritation. Carole was so kind and understanding. But Lisa still felt like a tagalong little sister, and the fact that she couldn't get Barq to lengthen bothered her more than she wanted to admit.

Lisa sighed. She was learning about sibling rivalry, all right, but this wasn't the way she would have chosen to learn.

STEVIE HEARD A soft tap on her bedroom door. "Go away!" she shouted. She yawned and stretched and turned the page of the book she was reading—*National Velvet*, for the three hundredth time.

Someone knocked again.

"Unless you're bringing me a hot fudge sundae, go away!"

The door opened. "It's me," Chad said.

"I'm honored," Stevie said, looking up briefly and going back to her book. "However, I have nothing whatsoever to say to you. Go away. And take that stupid soccer ball with you."

Chad quit bouncing the ball. He came in and wandered around Stevie's room. He picked up the model horses on her dresser and set them back down. He looked at her posters. He looked out the windows. He hummed to himself.

Stevie did her best to ignore him, but after a while it became impossible. "Are you deaf or stupid?" she asked. "I remember telling you to go away."

"You don't have to stay in your room all day," Chad said. "You just have to stay in the house. You could come downstairs."

"And hang out with you and Michael and Alex? No thanks. This is the one place where I've got my privacy." She glared at her brother. "Or *had* my privacy. Or thought I had. I'm getting a lock put on my door. That way cretinous, slimy brothers can't steal my riding boots in the middle of the night and—"

"Do you miss Belle?" Chad interrupted.

Stevie stared at him in amazement. He was even stupider than she'd thought. "Of course I miss Belle! You don't have any idea!" She pointed to Chad's soccer ball, now on her floor. "Imagine being separated from that ball of yours for two weeks, only imagine that the ball was alive, and happy to see you when you came to visit it. Imagine that you could ask it to do things and it would do them, and you could go places on it. Imagine that it was like a friend . . ." Stevie paused. "Oh, forget it. Unless you love horses, you'll never really understand." She lay back on her bed. "Now go away. You bug me."

Chad went over and picked up one of her model horses again. "I guess if Belle's like a friend, she probably misses you, too."

Stevie snorted. "Of course she misses me."

"Ummm-hmmm." Chad wiped the dust off the horse's nose. "I heard somewhere that horses pine," he commented casually. "What happens when they do that?"

Stevie studied Chad's back. He seemed entirely too casual to her. He was up to something. "Horses are social animals, see, and they make friendships that are really important to them. Like, if Starlight and Belle were stabled next to each other, they might become special buddies, even more so than they are already. Then if Belle moved away, Starlight would pine. He might not eat. He'd seem unhappy."

Chad nodded. He set the horse down and scooped up his soccer ball. "Just wondering," he said. When he was halfway out the door he paused, his hand on the frame. "Could horses pine for people, too?"

Stevie saw the hint of worry in Chad's eyes. "Of course," she said. "Horses pine for people even more than they pine for other horses. Now go away!"

MRS. LAKE SMILED at her four children all sitting quietly around the dinner table. "See what a pleasant meal it can be when no one argues?" she said. Stevie and her brothers exchanged glances. Since Stevie's disgrace, Chad, Alex, and Michael had been on their best behavior. None of them wanted to be grounded. Stevie thought they were all fiends. As soon as her punishment was over, she was going to get them, and good! She was making a list in her bedroom of ways to get revenge, and she was already on her third sheet of paper—in small handwriting.

But Lisa and Carole were working on a plan, and Stevie wasn't about to mess it up. She wiped her face with her napkin and set it carefully beside her plate. For another chance to go to camp, even she could behave for a week.

"Should I do the dishes?" she offered in a particularly well-behaved and pleasant voice.

"It's Chad's turn!" Stevie's twin, Alex, protested. Stevie couldn't help grinning. Alex was on her side in this one. Lately he hadn't been getting along with Chad, either.

"Yes, it is Chad's turn," Mr. Lake said. "Thank you for offering, though. I agree," he continued, turning to his wife, "this has been a remarkably pleasant meal. Maybe we should ground one or two of them all the time." He chuckled.

Stevie groaned. It was just like her father to pick the worst possible time to find a sense of humor. Why hadn't he been amused when Carole and the ladder had fallen into the pool?

The phone rang just as she was heading back upstairs. Her mother answered. "Oh, hi, Max!" Stevie heard her

68

say. Stevie paused at the foot of the stairs. Why was Max calling? Surely Lisa and Carole had explained about her being grounded—and anyway, she'd made the note for Belle's stall.

"Yes, okay," her mother said. "I'll tell her. Thank you, Max. Good-bye." Mrs. Lake hung up the phone. "Stevie?" she called. "That was Max. He said to tell you that Judy's coming out to look at Belle. He said you'd know about it—something about her mouth. It was a strange word he used. Is Belle having trouble eating? He said you'd understand."

Chad had stopped rinsing dishes the moment he heard his mother say "Max." He stood motionless while she relayed the message to Stevie.

"I understand, Mom," Stevie said. "Thanks."

Chad heard the stifled sob in her voice. Turning, he just managed to catch a glimpse of Stevie's face—pale and scared—before she ran up the stairs.

8

CAROLE STOPPED OUTSIDE Starlight's stall. "Good morning, you beautiful darling," she said. Starlight lifted his muzzle from his manger of grain. Seeing Carole, he took a few steps toward her and thrust his nose into her hands. "No carrots right now," Carole said, giving him a loving pat. Starlight didn't look disappointed; he simply went back to his breakfast.

Carole looked around her happily. In every stall, every horse was nose-deep in breakfast, content. Down the aisle Red had just wheeled the feeding cart back into its position under the grain chute. He waved to Carole and began filling buckets with water. It was early Tuesday morning, and everything was as it should be. All the horses looked great—including Belle. Stevie's mare looked as fresh as a summer flower. She poked her nose over her stall's half door and whinnied at Carole.

"Good morning to you, too," Carole said, laughing. "But you'll have to act less happy than that, you silly horse, if you want Stevie to take you to camp." Belle pricked her ears at the sound of Carole's voice. Max always said horses couldn't understand English. But that never stopped Carole from talking to them as if they could understand. She thought they liked to listen to friendly voices, just as they liked being groomed and fussed over.

"How does she look?" Lisa asked. Carole turned. Lisa was walking down the aisle holding a coffee mug carefully in her right hand. Over her left shoulder was a big canvas bag.

"Super," Carole said.

Lisa snorted. "Today, that's not necessarily good."

Carole grinned. She knew Lisa didn't mean she wanted Belle to be sick or unhappy. "If Belle's like Stevie," Carole said, "she's got enough of a dramatic instinct that she'll help us out."

Lisa laughingly agreed. They'd both said many times that Stevie had found a horse just like her.

71

Carole took the cup of coffee from Lisa and sniffed it. "Ooh, it smells awful strong!" She made a face. "That's wonderful! Where'd you get it?"

"My parents make a pot every morning. I just poured this cup once they went back upstairs to get dressed. They would have wondered if they'd seen me take some, since they know I'd never drink the stuff."

Carole nodded. Her father drank coffee, too, but since he never wanted more than a cup or two at once, he rarely made it at home.

"Is Belle finished with her breakfast yet?" Lisa asked, peering into the stall. The mare was licking the corners of her grain bucket, but all her grain seemed to be gone.

"Looks like she has," Carole answered. She set the coffee out of the way on a bench and took Belle out of her stall. While she gave Belle a quick grooming and picked the dirt out of her hooves, Lisa cleaned the stall.

"That's sort of a waste of time, considering," Lisa said as Carole picked up a body brush and started on Belle's coat.

"I know," Carole said, "but I can't help it. Besides, at least this way we've checked her over well." Lisa nodded. Carole brushed Belle's body and started on her legs. Grooming was good for a horse's coat and circulation, but it was also a great way to make sure the horse didn't have any hidden cuts, bumps, or sores. Belle was fine, but Carole knew there was always a small chance that the horse had injured herself in her stall overnight. She hadn't been lying when she'd told Chad that, with horses, serious problems were sometimes caused by minor things.

However, there was no evidence that Belle was pining for Stevie, injured, or in any other way less than perfectly fine. Carole put the thoroughly clean horse back into her thoroughly clean stall. Lisa poured a cupful of grain into Belle's empty bucket, and Carole poured the cold coffee over it. She mixed it in well.

Belle sniffed the grain curiously, then turned to the flake of hay on the floor by the door and began to eat that.

Carole gave a sigh of relief. "I was afraid she'd develop a taste for coffee overnight!" she joked.

"Nope," Lisa said in a satisfied voice. "She still hates it."

"Okay," Carole said. "Now for step two. Give me that bag of dirt, and you go talk to Chad."

LISA CHECKED HER WATCH as she approached Stevie's house. It was early enough that Chad probably hadn't left yet, but Stevie's parents certainly had. Lisa rang the doorbell.

"Hey, Lisa!" Davey, the college student watching the

young Lakes that summer, answered. Lisa noted with interest that he was starting to grow a tiny mustache. She liked Davey, but his mustache looked silly. He gave her an apologetic grin. "I know who you're here to see," he said. "Trust me, I completely sympathize, but I'm under strict orders not to let her have any visitors. I can give Stevie a message if you want."

"Thanks," Lisa said. "I'd like it if you'd tell her that Carole and I say hi. But I'm really here to see Chad."

Davey arched his eyebrows in surprise but opened the door wider and nodded. Lisa came in and sat down. In a few minutes Chad sauntered into the room, still wearing his soccer jersey. Lisa wondered if he ever wore any other clothes. She hoped he at least changed his socks sometimes.

She swallowed her disdain and put on her best expression of heartfelt concern. "Oh, Chad!" she said, jumping up and squeezing his hand. "I'm so glad you're home! We really need you!"

Chad yanked his hand back and looked wary. "Why?"

Lisa clasped her hands in front of her and let her dramatic silence speak for itself.

"It's Stevie's horse, isn't it?" Chad asked, his eyes widening. "She's still sick."

"I'm afraid so," Lisa said with an anguished sigh. "Carole and I are doing everything we can, but she's not

74

improving. In fact, she's getting worse. We think she needs companionship. Someone to take her mind off Stevie." Lisa gazed at him with what she hoped was an expression of sorrowful hope. "We need you to come sit with her for a while."

"Okay," Chad said, nodding.

Lisa stifled a shout of surprise. She couldn't believe it had been that easy!

"I'll come tonight, okay?"

"Oh. No, that won't work," Lisa said. She fought hard to think of an excuse. "See, Carole and I are staying with her, and so are some of Stevie's other friends, but right now we've got something else to do and no one can fill in. We need you now. Right now," she added.

Chad still looked concerned, but he frowned. "I can't come now! I've got a game this morning!"

Lisa shrugged. "Well, okay, I understand," she said, then gave a second small, sad shrug. "If one soccer game is more important to you than the life of your sister's beloved horse . . . sure, I understand. How many games do you have each week, anyway? Four? Five?"

"Only three," he answered. "Look, of course Belle is more important than a game—hey, I know, let's get Alex to sit with her now. I can do it later. You can put me on your schedule."

Lisa wondered if it would help if she started to cry.

She decided it wouldn't. She wasn't sure she could cry convincingly anyway. She wasn't *that* good an actress.

"I don't think Alex would help her," she said after a long pause. "He's almost never been to the barn. He doesn't understand horses at all. Horses can tell, you know, when people have empathy with them. You're the only person in your family besides Stevie who does. Remember?"

She desperately hoped he would remember his riding lessons but forget that he'd taken them because he had a crush on her. "Chad," she said beseechingly, "please." She put out her hand. Chad took a cautious step backward, as if to keep her from touching him again, but Lisa had no intention of doing so. By now his unwashed jersey was probably crawling with germs. She shuddered. "Belle needs you, Chad," she said. "She can't have Stevie. You're the next best thing."

Chad stared at her for what seemed like a very long time. "Okay," he said at last. "Wait here, and I'll go call my coach. I guess I can give up one game for Stevie."

"I know she'll be grateful," Lisa said.

"JUST SIT WITH HER for an hour or so," Lisa said as she led Chad into the stable. "Carole and I have an errand to run, but we'll be back just as soon as we possibly can."

In Belle's stall Carole was smoothing the last of the

76

fine dirt Lisa had brought into Belle's formerly glossy coat.

"How is she?" Lisa said. "Chad's here, Carole. You were right. He does care."

Carole looked up solemnly. "Thank you, Chad. I don't know, Lisa. See how dull her coat is? And I've been brushing her, too."

"So what if her coat's dull?" asked Chad. He patted Belle's nose a little uncertainly.

"It's one of the sure signs of illness," Carole informed him.

"Did she eat any grain?" Lisa asked anxiously, looking into the stall. What if Belle had!

Carole rattled the coffee-soaked grain in the bucket. "I'm afraid not."

Lisa noticed that all Belle's morning hay, however, was gone. The mare had made fast work of that—and with a full stomach, she wasn't likely to work up an appetite for her *café au grain*. Lisa let out a sigh of relief. "Well, there's not much anyone can do," she said. "But we'll keep doing all we can. Chad, just sit with her." They moved a hay bale next to Belle's stall door.

"Be her friend," Carole implored him. They walked sadly down the aisle and out of the stable, leaving Chad alone with the poor, sick horse.

*   *   *

CAROLE SLID INTO their favorite booth at TD's, Willow Creek's best ice cream parlor and a Saddle Club hangout. "It's a little early for a sundae, don't you think?"

Lisa thought hard before replying. "No. I don't."

Their usual waitress set water glasses down in front of them. "Where's your partner in crime?" she asked them.

"Grounded," Carole answered.

The waitress grinned. "She earned it, I'm sure." She handed them menus and walked away.

Lisa stared after her. "What a thing to say!"

Carole was laughing. "She's right, you know."

"Still, she doesn't have to be so bitter. It's not like Stevie orders weird sundaes just to get on the waitress's bad side."

When they were deeply involved in the enjoyment of two hot fudge brownie sundaes, Carole said, "I think it's working. I think this plan of yours is going to work."

"Maybe," Lisa said, scooping a pecan off the top of her ice cream. "The only catch is, we're relying on him to have a conscience."

Carole grinned. "He's got one. I'm telling you, I've got this whole sibling thing figured out."

Lisa grinned in return. She was beginning to feel that she, too, had the whole sibling thing figured out. The night before, it had occurred to her that she wouldn't have been nearly as upset about her riding if Carole and Stevie had been having trouble, too. She had been competing with them whether she'd realized it or not.

"So," Carole asked, "which horse are you going to ride in our lesson this afternoon? Will Max let you have Prancer?"

Lisa thought, not for the first time, that Carole must be able to read her mind. "Max said this morning that he'd let me have Prancer," she said. "But I told him I'd rather ride Barq. I know that sounds strange," she added hastily, before Carole could say anything, "but after all I am taking Prancer to camp, and Barq and I came so close yesterday that I just don't want to give up with him until we get that exercise right." She scooped up a bite of ice cream. "You think I'm silly, don't you?" she asked. "When I could be riding the horse I love?"

Carole smiled warmly. "I don't think you're silly at all," she said. She thought about saying more, about how important she thought it was that Lisa not give up with Barq, and how much Lisa could learn from riding different types of horses, but she decided not to. From Lisa's outburst the day before, Carole had gathered that her friend needed support but probably didn't want to hear much advice.

Carole set her spoon down in her empty dish. "You

were right, it wasn't too early for a sundae. But we'd better get back. If we wait too long, Belle might get hungry enough to snack on that grain."

"Wait," Lisa said. "You've got fudge sauce on your chin." She handed Carole her napkin. "What about me?"

Carole inspected her. "You're clean."

CHAD WAS SITTING on a hay bale outside Belle's stall, but when he saw them he stood up right away. "She hasn't eaten," he said. "I even took the grain out of the bucket and tried to stick it in her mouth, but she wouldn't eat it. She didn't seem to like it at all."

Carole tried not to laugh at her mental image of Chad poking grain between Belle's lips.

"Poor Belle," murmured Lisa.

Carole pressed her lips tight together. She would not laugh. They observed the suffering horse in silence.

"Lisa and I can walk you home," Carole offered at last. She needed to get away from bright-eyed Belle before she had hysterics. His riding lessons obviously hadn't taught Chad much about horses if he really believed this one was sick. Carole wouldn't have been fooled for a moment. Belle's coat was dull, sure, but it looked *dirty*.

"You're not both going to leave her, are you?" Chad

asked anxiously. "Can someone else watch her? I mean, she hasn't eaten at all."

"I'll stay with her," Lisa said. "You're totally right, someone should, and I don't think anyone else is scheduled for this morning."

Carole's eyebrows rose. " 'Scheduled'?" she mouthed behind Chad's back.

"Thank you, Chad," Lisa continued. "I'm sure you've made a difference. She may not have gotten better, but at least she hasn't gotten any worse."

Carole turned away. Lisa and Chad could see her shoulders quivering. "I'm sorry," Carole said, choking.

"She'll be okay," Chad said, desperately trying to comfort Carole. He'd certainly never seen Carole Hanson cry!

"I'll watch her now," Lisa commanded. "You two go." She had to get Carole out of here before she ruined everything. Carole was just about to explode with laughter.

Chad heard the urgency in Lisa's voice and understood that she didn't want Carole upset any further. "Let's go," he said gently. He put his hand on Carole's shoulder and guided her down the aisle. Carole, overcome, covered her face with her hands.

Lisa steeled herself against a similar outburst. *It wouldn't be so funny,* she thought, *if he weren't swallowing everything, hook, line, and sinker.* They had Chad completely in their power. She grabbed a brush and began to clean the dirt off Belle.

"IT'LL BE OKAY," Chad repeated for perhaps the hundredth time as they walked up the sidewalk toward the Lakes' house. Carole nodded. She still didn't trust herself to speak.

"Look," Chad continued, pointing to the second story of the house, "there's Stevie waving."

Carole waved back. As they came closer, she could see the anxious expression on Stevie's face. Stevie opened her window and sailed a paper airplane down.

Chad looked over Carole's shoulder as she unfolded it. *Why a vet?* the note said. *Is Belle sick?*

Chad looked at Carole. Carole felt her stomach drop. What could she possibly say? She didn't want to make Stevie think there was something wrong with Belle—she knew how much it would worry Stevie. And yet Chad was watching. So far, he believed them.

Carole bit her lip. Finally she called up to the window, "She's not eating."

Carole hoped Stevie would be content with that much of an explanation, but she didn't really expect that she would be. After all, if something was wrong with Starlight, Carole would demand to know all the details.

So Carole wasn't really surprised when, a moment later, a second airplane flew out of Stevie's window. *Colic?* it read.

Carole shrugged unhappily. Chad watched her, his hands on his hips. "We're afraid it might be," Carole said at last, even though her heart was breaking at the thought of what she was doing to Stevie. Stevie gasped. She shut her eyes, slammed the window down, and backed away, disappearing from view.

"You didn't have a choice," Chad told Carole solemnly. "She deserves to know the truth."

Carole walked miserably back to Pine Hollow. Stevie deserved the truth, all right—and Carole had told her a lie.

Chad walked into his house. He stopped in the entryway. Even from so far away, he could hear his sister's sobs.

9

"LISA?" MAX STUCK HIS HEAD out of his office door just as Lisa walked into the stable. "Did you remember that Judy's coming to do Belle's teeth this morning?"

"Of course," Lisa said. "That's why I'm here so early. Carole and I are both going to help."

Max smiled. "Great. I've got an early lesson, so I can't attend to it, though I'm sure my mom or Red could have if you two couldn't. But it's a good chance to learn something, especially since you said you'd never seen teeth floated before."

Lisa grimaced. "It seems like everything is a good

84

chance to learn something," she complained. "I never quit learning!"

Max came out of his office. He crossed his arms and spoke to her seriously. "I agree it gets frustrating sometimes," he said. "But I think one of the truly wonderful things about horses is that they've always got something new to teach us, if we stay willing to learn. No one can ever know everything about horses.

"In fact," he continued with a small grin, "sometimes I used to feel just the way you probably do—as though someday, if I tried hard enough, I could know everything. Then I got a chance to talk to one of Nigel Hawthorne's friends. At the time, this friend was the top-ranked event rider in the entire world."

"Wow," Lisa said softly. Nigel was a world-class rider, and they'd all gone to several events to watch him ride. Lisa could hardly imagine anyone being a better rider than Nigel.

"Yes," Max said, "and that man, the champion, told me that every day he learned something new. He'd ridden on four Olympic teams, and he said he still hoped that someday he'd learn how to be a really good rider. So don't give in to your discouragement, Lisa. You can't know everything, but you have learned a lot."

"But that's not my problem, Max," Lisa protested. "I don't want to know *everything*. I just want to know more than Stevie and Carole do." As soon as she said it she felt shocked. How could she feel that way about her best friends? But she did!

Max didn't look shocked. He gave her face a gentle pat. "I know," he said. "But you can't control that—you can't change what Stevie and Carole know. All you can do is keep improving yourself. You made a good start with that yesterday, when you did so well in your lesson with Barq. You really learned lengthening, Lisa, and you might not have, at least not so completely, if you hadn't had to struggle with it for a while."

"I guess," Lisa said, smiling at the memory of finally, finally, sailing through those wide-spaced poles without a single whack. "I'm glad you understand, Max. I don't really want to be better than Stevie or Carole—and yet I do."

"That's okay," Max said. "Just keep things in perspective, all right? It's not often I have a student who learns as quickly as you." He looked up as they heard a sudden noise in the driveway. "There's Judy's truck, and my student's car."

"And Carole," Lisa said, seeing her friend walk up the driveway. Carole usually took a bus from her house to a stop near Pine Hollow. Lisa went to greet her friend, comforted by the fact that Max seemed to understand her feelings. *A horse of my own would help*, she thought,

86

but I still wouldn't know as much as Carole. About horses, anyway, she corrected herself. *I probably know more about ballet.*

"Hey, Carole, do you know what a *battement tendu* is?" she asked as Carole came closer. She smiled mischievously at the look of bewilderment on her friend's face. "This!" She elevated herself on one foot and tapped the other gracefully around her ankle.

"Okay," Carole said, giving Lisa a puzzled look. "What's it for?"

"Nothing, I just wondered if you knew." Lisa lifted her chin, moved her arms into a graceful *port des bras*, and carried herself down the stable aisle on *demi-pointes*. "We'd better get Belle out for Judy."

CAROLE HELD BELLE on a lead rope in the center aisle. "It's best not to put her on cross-ties for something like this," she explained to Lisa. "If she decides to protest and flips her head back hard enough, she could flip herself over. The cross-ties would break, of course, but she could hurt herself, and besides, it's easier to control her with the lead rope."

"Uh-huh," Lisa said, nodding. She was examining the long tools that Judy would use to file Belle's teeth. They looked, she decided, like short snow-shovel handles with cheese graters attached to the end. One file was for coarsely grated cheese, the other for fine. Lisa knew she wouldn't want those things anywhere near her teeth.

Carole grimaced. Here she was, running off at the mouth again! No wonder Lisa didn't like it.

Lisa looked up and caught the expression on Carole's face. "It's okay," she said. "In the first place, I didn't know that, and in the second place, I know you can't help yourself. You shouldn't have to try. It's the way you are. I like the way you are. You're one of my best friends." She smiled, and Carole smiled back in relief.

Judy opened Belle's mouth and felt deeply along the long, narrow sides of her jaw. "Yep, she's got some points back there," she said. "Stevie was right. She was really paying attention."

"Couldn't she have checked Belle herself?" Lisa asked.

"Probably not," Carole said. "Her molars are way back behind the space where the bit rests. It's a long reach. Anyway, Judy's the expert."

Judy grinned. She knew The Saddle Club well, especially Carole, who sometimes accompanied her on her rounds. "Yes, I'm quite an expert, all right," she said, laughing at her own joke. "This is a job for Supervet! But I left my cape at home."

Lisa held up one of the files. "And this thing really doesn't hurt?"

"It doesn't hurt," Judy said. "Horses don't have any

feeling in the points of their teeth, any more than you do in the tips of your nails, and even though those files look like something out of the Middle Ages, they do their job well. On the other hand, the files make a lot of noise, and, as you'll see, bits of tooth go flying. Some horses hate it, even though it doesn't hurt. If I remember right, Belle didn't like this the last time."

Belle didn't like it this time, either. She threw her head up the moment Judy approached with the file, and she pulled Carole backward halfway down the aisle. All Judy's soothing words and gentle movements weren't enough to change Belle's mind.

"Just like I remembered," Judy said. "The thing to do here, girls, is give her a little tranquilizer. It'll make things easier and safer for all of us." She gave Belle an injection in her hip, and a few minutes later the horse was swaying woozily, her head hanging near her knees.

"Wow," said Lisa, impressed. "That stuff really acted fast."

"Yes, and it'll go away fast, too. In an hour she'll be completely back to normal." Judy lifted Belle's head and began again with the coarse file. Belle still pulled away slightly, but the spirit of resistance had left her. In a very short time her teeth were done.

"There, now she'll be much more comfortable," Judy said, giving Belle a pat. "Go ahead and leave her in her stall, girls, but take out her food if she has any left. You don't want her eating until the tranq's worn off. Her muscles are so relaxed that she could choke."

Judy stepped back and admired Belle as Lisa put her back into her stall. "She's really in tip-top shape, isn't she? Stevie takes great care of her. I hope Stevie's back riding soon. Max told me the story."

"All of it?" Carole asked.

"All," Judy said. "Your midnight swim and everything." She winked. "But I feel sorry for her, I do. Especially because of camp." She finished packing her bags and left the stable.

Lisa leaned over the edge of Belle's door. The mare was standing with her face to the wall, head drooping, hind leg slack. She looked truly wretched. Lisa had a hard time believing that Belle would be perfectly normal within the hour. "We should go get Chad right now," she said to Carole. *Before the tranquilizer wears off,* she added to herself. Who would have guessed that Belle would need one? Judy said most horses didn't.

"You don't need to get me," a voice said near Lisa's ear. "I'm right here."

Lisa jumped so quickly that she hit her elbow on the side of the stall. "Chad! I—I didn't see you standing there." Frantically she tried to remember what she had just said to Carole. Had she said the word *tranquilizer* out loud?

"I just wanted to check on her, to see if she was any better than she was yesterday," Chad said.

"See for yourself," Carole offered, stepping out of Chad's way.

He peered into Belle's stall. He was wearing, Lisa noted with interest, a different soccer jersey. But his socks were definitely the same as yesterday's. Lisa recognized the ladderlike run in the back of the left one.

"Maybe you need to do some laundry," she suggested.

"Gosh," Chad said, intent on the horse, "she looks worse. A whole lot worse!"

"It's a progressive condition, you know," Lisa informed him.

"The vet just left," Carole added.

Chad nodded. "I know. I saw her truck. I tried to wave her down so I could ask her about Belle, but she just waved back and kept driving."

Lisa offered a small prayer of thanks for that. "I'm afraid Belle's much worse," she said softly. "It's no more than we expected, though. We've done all we can."

"Her coat looks a lot shinier, though," Chad noted. Lisa and Carole exchanged quick glances.

"Uh . . ." Lisa fumbled for a reason. *We washed the*

dirt off her? That wouldn't go over well! "It's a false bloom," she said at last. "Like in those old books, when people are dying of tuberculosis and their cheeks get all red. They begin to look healthy again just before . . . before the end."

"You think she's got tuberculosis?" Chad sounded truly alarmed.

"No, no—"

"Lisa was just making a comparison," Carole said. She added thoughtfully, "I don't think horses get tuberculosis."

"Well, that's good," Chad said, "or Belle would probably have it."

Lisa and Carole didn't know what to make of that statement, so they ignored it. The three of them watched Belle in silence for a while. The mare shifted her weight slowly between her two front feet.

"Is she eating?" Chad asked.

"No," Lisa said mournfully. "Judy took her grain away. She said it could only hurt her, in the condition she's in."

"Wow." Chad sounded impressed.

Another long silence ensued. Lisa began to wonder how they could get Chad to leave. If the tranquilizer wore off while he was watching, it would look like a medical miracle.

"We've got to do something," Chad said at last. "What do you think she needs? What'll make her better?"

"Only one thing," Carole intoned in a deep, mysterious voice she'd picked up from watching fifties horror movies late at night with her father. "Stevie."

Chad nodded. "I know," he whispered. "I just don't know how to get her here. My parents are still really upset. Maybe there's something else we could do." He looked up, and his face brightened. "Maybe," he said, "we could ask Mrs. Reg."

Carole and Lisa whirled around. Lisa tried to conceal the expression of horror that she knew was spreading across her face. Mrs. Reg, of all people, was coming down the stable aisle, heading straight for them! There was no escape. Lisa's plan was ruined. Mrs. Reg would not for one second believe that Belle had so much as a mosquito bite, let alone advanced colic.

It was like, Carole thought, being trapped inside one of those late-night films. The aliens were coming to get you, and your feet couldn't move. You couldn't even scream. You could only watch, in horror, as your life— or, in this case, Stevie's trip to camp—ended in horrible, oozing death. Mrs. Reg was not going to find their scheme amusing. Furthermore, she'd been nearby when Judy had given Belle the tranquilizer.

93

"Mrs. Reg," Chad said, beckoning earnestly, seemingly oblivious to the two girls' expressions, "Belle's really sick! She looks like she's dying! We've got to do something!"

"Let's see," Mrs. Reg said briskly. She came to Belle's stall, looked inside, and then opened the door and went in. She ran her hands over Belle's body, lifted her head, checked her gums, and looked carefully at her eyes.

Lisa wished an earthquake would come along and swallow her on the spot. Carole wondered why the monstrous space aliens never swallowed their victims whole. They always finished them off slowly, bit by agonizing bit.

Mrs. Reg ran her hands down Belle's legs. Chad watched her with an expression of anxious hope. Lisa and Carole looked at each other. They both knew there was no hope.

Mrs. Reg stood up and came out of the stall. She looked at them solemnly. Lisa felt her heart skip a beat. Carole knew this was the end.

"Poor baby," Mrs. Reg said softly, with a sad shake of her head. "I'm afraid there's nothing anyone can do. She's dying of a broken heart."

Lisa's heart skipped a beat again, for an entirely different reason. Carole wondered how often the space aliens turned out to be heroes—heroines?—in disguise.

94

Mrs. Reg gave Chad's arm a sympathetic pat. Without a glance at the girls, she sailed back down the aisle, went into her office, and closed the door.

Lisa clutched the top of the stall in pure relief. Carole struggled not to laugh. Chad looked downcast. "I guess it's really serious, then," he said. Carole, still unable to speak, nodded solemnly, while Lisa averted her eyes.

10

"STEVIE! STEPHANIE! Stephanie Lake, come down here, please!"

Stevie jumped at the sound of her mother's voice. *National Velvet* slid off her chest onto the floor, and she sat up and absentmindedly put it back on the bed, where she had been lying. She must have fallen asleep. She'd been dreaming of herself and Belle, sailing over Beecher's Brook, winning the Grand National, the hardest steeplechase in all the world—Belle, the horse nobody wanted, and herself only a slip of a girl . . .

"Stephanie Lake!" Stevie blinked. Her mother called

her Stephanie only when something serious was going on. But what was her mother doing home in the middle of a Wednesday afternoon?

"Coming!" Stevie yelled.

"This had better be serious, young man," Stevie heard her father's voice say. Her father? What was he doing home?

Suddenly Stevie felt very curious. She paused just a moment at her mirror—making sure she looked suitably tragic and afflicted—and hurried downstairs.

Chad was standing in the entryway, holding his shoulders carefully square and his hands tight behind his back. He looked terrified—so terrified, in fact, that Stevie felt a rush of sympathy for him, until she remembered how her pink flowered underwear had looked hanging from the flagpole, waving in the warm summer breeze. No, Chad deserved whatever he was about to get.

Stevie sniffed sadly and slumped her shoulders. Her mother came briskly out of the living room. "There you are, honey," she said. "Your brother asked us to come home. He says he needs to talk to all of us, including you."

Stevie's dad opened the door of his home office. "Come inside," he commanded. He shut the door after them. Stevie heard it click and felt a satisfied thrill. Her dad shut the door only when they were in serious trouble. For once Stevie knew she hadn't done anything wrong. Chad must be quaking in his boots—or in his smelly soccer shoes.

"So," Mrs. Lake said conversationally, taking a seat in the wing chair, "what was so important, Chad, that I had to cancel my afternoon meetings and come home? I expected broken bones at least."

"Well," Chad said. "Well, see . . ." His voice squeaked an octave higher, and he paused. Mr. Lake sat down behind his desk and swiveled to face his children, and as he did, Stevie caught the brief, amused look that passed between her parents. They weren't truly angry, she realized. They were *pretending* to be angry. How odd.

Stevie didn't think that had ever happened before. Chad, however, didn't appear to have caught on. He looked genuinely anxious.

"Stevie can't be grounded anymore," he said. "You've got to unground her now, right away." He spoke in a rush, his words tumbling out, as he shifted his weight nervously back and forth on the carpet. Stevie felt a flood of absolute joy. She tried hard not to show it.

"Chad," his mother interrupted, "are you wearing your cleats?"

Chad looked down and swallowed hard. He quickly removed his soccer shoes and used his toe to scrub away the indentations they had left in the plush carpet.

98

"She can't be grounded anymore," he repeated.

"Why not?" Mr. Lake was a trial lawyer, and it showed in his tone of voice. He sounded as if he were interrogating a hostile witness.

"Because some stuff was my fault, too," Chad said. "It wasn't just Stevie."

"What stuff? What wasn't just Stevie's fault?"

Chad shrugged uncomfortably. "All those pranks and stuff. I mean, Stevie did them, but so did I."

Stevie coughed to hide a grin. This was turning out great—better than she'd hoped.

"And what exactly did you do?" Mr. Lake picked up a pencil and twisted it between his fingers. Stevie had been to court a few times to watch her father work. This was what he looked like there. If it hadn't been for her flying-flag underwear, and her riding boots, and most especially camp, she would almost have felt sorry for Chad.

"I put whipped cream in her riding boots," Chad confessed. He had started off with the most minor prank, Stevie noted. The whipped cream hadn't been hard to wipe out.

"Is that all?"

"No—"

"What else?"

"I refilled her shampoo bottle with chocolate syrup,"

Chad said. Stevie flinched at the memory. The syrup had *not* been easy to wash out.

"Goodness, Chad," Mrs. Lake said lightly. "You filled Stevie's room with popcorn, too. I don't know if we should let you have any more food."

"What else?" Mr. Lake interjected sternly.

Chad squirmed. There was silence. "I glued the pages of her horse magazine together," he said.

"What else?"

"I hung her underwear on the flagpole. But she turned my underwear pink!"

"It was an accident!" Stevie cut in. "I did his laundry! I was trying to do him a favor!"

"Oh, right, some favor," Chad said sarcastically. "Like you didn't do it on purpose."

"What else?" Mr. Lake continued, in a louder voice. Stevie shut up fast. "Chad?"

Chad sighed. He seemed determined to make a full confession. "When you yelled at Michael last week for letting his bathwater slop all over the carpet, the water was really from a bucket I stuck over Stevie's door. It just sort of sloshed across the hall." He paused. Stevie figured that was all he was going to say. She knew she would never admit to more than that.

But Chad continued. "The night Stevie got the ladder and was spying in my bedroom, Mark and I were going

100

to use Super Glue to stick the little plastic horses from my old toy soldier set all over the tops of her boots. It was my idea," he added hastily. "Not Mark's. It wasn't his fault. But see, Stevie saw us, and that's why she started yelling, and that's why she crashed into the flowers and stuff. And I put her boots back and I forgot to mention that they'd been in my room—" He glanced at Stevie. "I mean, I lied about it. So it wasn't her fault. So she has to be ungrounded, right now. *Please*. It's really important." He shuffled his stocking feet. Stevie noticed the run down the back of his left sock. Hadn't he worn those socks the day before?

Mrs. Lake held up a finger. "Just for clarification," she asked, "which pair of Stevie's boots did you take? Her old snow boots?"

Chad shook his head miserably. "Her riding boots," he whispered.

"Her *new* riding boots? The ones she got for her birthday?"

Chad nodded. Stevie felt herself growing furious about it all over again. At least her pranks weren't mean—except, maybe, for the tacks in Chad's shoes.

"Her *expensive* riding boots?" Mrs. Lake continued. "You were going to put Super Glue on those?" Chad nodded again. "Well," said his mother, "if I had seen you do that, I would have started screaming at you myself.

The popcorn prank was funny, Chad. It was out of line, but it was funny, and it didn't hurt anything. This is different. It's destructive. I won't tolerate it. Do you understand?"

Chad mumbled.

"Excuse me?" Mrs. Lake said.

"Yes," Chad said. "I do understand. And I'm really sorry, believe me." He turned toward his sister. "I'm sorry, Stevie," he said.

"Okay," Stevie said. "I'm sorry about the tacks in your shoes." To her mother she added, "I'm sorry about the flowers, too, but you know I didn't wreck them on purpose. I know how much you loved those pansies." The garden shops didn't sell pansies in late summer, so Stevie had had to plant geraniums in that bed.

Mr. Lake tapped his desk pad with his pencil. "What's the point of all this, Chad?" he asked. "Much as your mother and I appreciate your confession, you had gotten away with everything. Why tell us about it now?"

Chad bit his lip. "I went to Pine Hollow yesterday, and again today," he said. "Stevie's horse is really sick. She misses Stevie so much, she's dying. If she doesn't see Stevie soon, she's really going to die. And I know how much Stevie loves Belle. I don't want Belle's blood on my hands. I'm sorry. I had to tell you. You have to let

Stevie see her horse." His voice rose anxiously with the last words.

Stevie tried to look sorrowful all over again, and shocked, as if Belle's illness were a complete surprise.

Mr. Lake's stern expression changed. His lips twitched, and his eyebrows arched in disbelief. "Stevie's horse is dying?" he repeated.

"I know it sounds weird, but she is," Chad persisted. "Mrs. Reg said so. She said poor Belle was dying of a broken heart." His voice trembled with earnestness.

"Oh, Chad, I really doubt—" his mother began.

"Mrs. Reg said so! And I saw Belle. She looks it, too!"

Stevie's parents looked at each other. There was a long silence. Stevie struggled to keep a suitably solemn face. She held her breath.

"Well," Mrs. Lake said at last, "we hope you two have learned a lesson."

Chad nodded and said yes. Stevie didn't say anything.

"These constant pranks have absolutely got to stop," Mrs. Lake continued. "On the other hand—"

Stevie exhaled. She'd been so hoping there was an other hand.

"—On the other hand, Stevie, you've behaved well during your punishment. You haven't tried to sneak out to Pine Hollow, you haven't tried to call your friends, and you've behaved civilly to the rest of us, even though it appears you had reason to be angry at Chad. Also, the flowers look nice, and I know you paid for your share of them and the screen door."

Stevie nodded. Her piggy bank would never be the same.

"So you seem to have been punished enough," her father said. He turned to Chad. "However, in view of your recent testimony, young man, you don't seem to have been punished enough. Do you agree?"

Chad hung his head. "I guess so."

"Good. Admission of guilt allows for leniency in sentencing. You're grounded, Chad, but only for four days."

"Starting when?" Chad asked. Stevie knew he had two soccer games on Saturday.

"Starting now."

"What about me?" Stevie asked.

Her parents smiled at each other. "You're ungrounded," Mrs. Lake said. "Starting now."

Even though after all this Stevie had been expecting her mother to say that, she could still hardly believe it. "You mean it?" she asked. "I can go to camp?"

Mr. Lake smiled. "You can go to camp."

"Yippeeee!" Stevie jumped in the air. Chad grabbed her by the arm.

"You've got to get to Pine Hollow!" he urged her. "Hurry! Right away!"

Stevie looked at her parents, who nodded. She dashed for the office door. Then she stopped and turned. Chad looked so worried about Belle. He'd looked so worried the whole time he was talking to their parents. He'd done all this for her.

Stevie was surprised at herself, but suddenly she felt she didn't want Chad to worry anymore. "Can Chad come with me to Pine Hollow?" she asked. "Just so he can see how Belle is doing now?"

Stevie's parents looked as surprised as she felt. "Okay," her mother said after a pause. "But on your honor, Chad. Come straight home when you're through. You'll be grounded as soon as you get back."

"Thanks!" Chad said. He struggled into his shoes, then beat Stevie to the front door. "C'mon! We don't have any time to lose!"

11

STEVIE KNEW SHE WAS in pretty good shape, but with all the soccer Chad played he easily outran her to Pine Hollow. He was waiting outside the stable door when Stevie got there, breathing hard. "Just a minute!" she gasped. "Let me get my breath." Chad pounded her on the back while she bent over and coughed.

"Okay." Stevie stood and looked around her. After her four-day absence, Pine Hollow seemed more beautiful than ever before. For a moment Stevie let her gaze wander over the lovely riding ring, the beautiful horses grazing in the pasture, the indoor arena, the manure pile,

Max's ancient, rusted-out truck . . . it all looked so amazingly wonderful. Stevie drew in a deep, pleased breath. She was so glad to be back.

"C'mon," Chad said. "Belle needs you!"

"Oh, right." Stevie went into the stable. "Belle!" she cried out. "Belle! Belle! Here I come!"

From around the corner came Belle's high-pitched whinny. Stevie began to grin. How she had missed that sound!

"She hears you!" Chad said. He broke into a run.

"Hey!" Stevie called after him. "No running in the stable!" It was a safety rule. Also, Stevie wanted to savor the moment. While Chad hopped up and down impatiently, Stevie walked slowly around the corner.

"Oh, Belle!" Despite herself, Stevie ran the last few steps to her mare's stall. Belle had indeed heard Stevie's voice and responded. She had thrust her head and neck over the half door of the stall and was looking eagerly, ears up and eyes bright, down the aisle in the direction of Stevie's voice. When she saw Stevie, she began to bob her head and whicker.

Stevie threw her arms around Belle's neck. "Oh, my sweet, darling horse," she crooned. "Did you miss me? I missed you!" Belle nuzzled Stevie's shirt. Stevie buried her face in Belle's neck and breathed in the rich, wonderful smell of her horse.

"It's a miracle!" Stevie opened her eyes. Chad was staring thunderstruck at Belle. "A miracle, Stevie!" he repeated, wide-eyed. "If you saw what she looked like this morning—she's so much better now. It's unbelievable."

He patted Belle softly on the nose, his eyes wide with wonderment. "Gee, Lisa and Carole were right all along. They said Belle needed you. They were right. Look at her. She's been cured by love."

"She's beautiful," Stevie said. She was so happy to see Belle that at that exact moment she would have given Chad her new riding boots, gladly, and let him fill them to their tops with whipped cream or sour cream or whatever, and glue whole herds of plastic horses on them, in exchange for being with her beloved horse again. Not to mention being able to go to camp. Stevie loved her brother as she never had before.

Of course, she reflected, the whole mess had really been his fault all along. If he hadn't been such a brat, she wouldn't have needed to spy on him.

"Do you think we should give her some grain?" Chad asked eagerly.

"Sure," Stevie said. "A little extra won't hurt her."

"Extra?" Chad looked puzzled. "But she's hardly been eating at all, Stevie. It's not extra."

"I mean," Stevie amended, "it won't hurt her to have a little in the middle of the afternoon. Sure."

They went together to the feed room and got half a scoop of grain. Chad very carefully poured it into the bucket in Belle's stall. Belle dived for it. She seemed delighted at the unexpected treat.

"She's eating!" Chad said.

"Yay!" Stevie cheered. Belle looked up briefly at the noise, then went back to the grain.

"I just can't believe how much better she looks," Chad said. "Yesterday her coat was all dark, and this morning she looked almost unconscious."

"I was really worried about her," Stevie said, stroking Belle's shining neck. "Yesterday, when Carole said it could be colic—that was bad."

"I heard you crying," Chad said.

Stevie looked at her brother. Most of the time she detested him, but every once in a while . . . "That was a really nice thing you did, Chad," she said. "Making Mom and Dad come home in the afternoon, and telling them about everything you did."

Chad blushed. "I was afraid to wait until dinner," he said. "It might have been too late for Belle by then. Anyway, I didn't do much. All I did was tell the truth."

"Which was probably more than I would have done," Stevie said in a sudden burst of honesty.

"Even if my horse was dying? If I had a horse, or something else I loved as much as you loved Belle, and it was dying, don't you think you would have done the same thing for me?"

"Maybe," Stevie admitted. She smiled. "I might have, but you did. Thank you, Chad. Now Belle's okay, and I get to go to camp and everything. Thank you, very much."

"You're welcome." Chad looked at Stevie with a shy smile. "Don't hug me or anything, okay? People could be watching."

Stevie nodded. "As long as you promise not to hug me, either," she said.

"IT'S BEAUTIFUL," Carole said mistily. "Like the happy ending of a movie. Two sworn enemies declaring their secret, undying love for one another . . . it almost chokes me up."

"Almost," Lisa said. "Not quite. I agree with the sworn enemies part, but 'undying love'? I think what Stevie and Chad have is more like secret, undying tolerance."

"Still, look at them!"

Lisa looked, peeking through a large crack between

the boards of Barq's stall. She and Carole had been helping Red clean stalls when they heard Stevie and Chad enter the barn. As quickly as they could, they'd hidden themselves in the stall they were cleaning. Luckily, it was across the aisle and only a little way down from Belle's stall. They'd been able to see all of Stevie's joyful reunion with her horse.

Now Stevie and Chad were talking earnestly, in soft voices Lisa couldn't quite hear. She strained her ears. "She gets to go to camp!" she told Carole at last.

"All right!" Carole whispered. She and Lisa exchanged quick hugs of delight.

"Our plan worked," Lisa said. "I can't believe it. Shhh! Let's hear what else they're saying." She and Carole waited in silence, but most of the rest of Stevie and Chad's conversation was too quiet for them to catch. All they could hear was Chad saying, "Don't hug me or anything."

"Just like a boy," Lisa said in disgust.

"More like a brother than a boy," Carole corrected her with a smile. "I told you, I've got this sibling thing figured out."

"I'm glad at least one of us does," Lisa said. She sat down in the clean sawdust in the stall. Now that she knew Stevie would be able to go to camp, she wasn't much interested in the rest of her conversation with

Chad. Camp with Stevie was all that mattered. *No,* Lisa corrected herself, *make that camp with Stevie and Prancer.*

"We're quite a team," Carole said softly, sitting down beside Lisa. "I figure out the sibling thing, you make the plan."

"We out-Stevied Stevie," Lisa said with satisfaction. "We made a scheme all our own, and it worked."

Carole looked at Lisa and shook her head. "You made the scheme," she said. "*You* out-Stevied Stevie, not me." Lisa looked up, surprised and doubtful. Carole continued. "I mean it. You're the one who thought of everything in the first place. You came up with the dirt idea, and the coffee, and you convinced Chad that we were serious. All I did was follow your lead."

The two girls looked at each other. "Did it bother you?" Lisa asked at last.

"No," Carole said, "because I thought your idea was good." She thought for a moment. "No, that isn't true. It did bother me a little, Lisa—just a very little bit. You're so smart, you always get As in school, and sometimes I wish I could figure things out as fast as you do."

"The way I sometimes wish I knew as much about horses as you do," Lisa answered.

"Exactly."

Lisa felt a sudden flush of happiness. At first she thought it was because she'd finally done something Carole couldn't do. Then she realized she was happy because she finally understood that Carole felt the same way she did. Carole sounded just a little bit—well, *envious* of Lisa. And that made Lisa glad because it made her own envy seem less wicked.

She smiled. "It's a little bit like being sisters, isn't it?"

Carole stretched, yawned, and smiled. "Yes, and, girl, I'm telling you, I've got this sibling thing figured out!"

Lisa rolled onto her knees and pressed her face against the crack in the wall. "Chad's gone," she announced.

Carole knelt beside her. Across the aisle, Stevie was fastening Belle's halter behind her ears. While they watched, Stevie carefully smoothed Belle's mane and forelock away from the leather. Stevie snapped her lead rope onto the halter, opened Belle's door, and started to lead her from the stall. Before they had gone two steps Stevie stopped and threw her arms around Belle's neck. Stevie's face shined with pure joy.

In the stall, Lisa reached for Carole's hand and squeezed it. She knew Carole was right—her plan had reunited Stevie and Belle. Lisa finally felt the equal of the rest of The Saddle Club again.

12

STEVIE GAVE BELLE another hug and a pat. After having been away so long, she didn't think she could ever hug her horse enough. Then she took Belle out of her stall and fastened her to the cross-ties.

"Come out, come out, wherever you are," she called. "Carole, Lisa, I know you're here somewhere. Guess what? I'm not grounded anymore!"

Giggling, Carole and Lisa rushed out of Barq's stall and hugged Stevie. "Hooray!" Lisa said. "We're so glad to see you!"

"And talk to you," Carole added. "No more paper airplanes. But how did you know we were here?"

Stevie shrugged. "Where else would you be? Starlight was in his stall, so I knew you weren't out on a trail ride. Plus, I thought I heard someone—two someones—whispering."

"We weren't exactly trying to eavesdrop," Carole said. "I mean, we didn't think you'd be having a really private conversation with Chad—"

"—but we couldn't help overhearing—" Lisa said.

"—that I'm going to camp!" Stevie finished. After a round of celebratory high fives, she added, "And you two were great—fantastic!"

"We tried to take good care of Belle," Carole assured her. "We groomed her every day and made sure she was turned out in the pasture. But the important thing is, she's not sick at all." Carole could feel her face flush. "Stevie, I am so, so sorry for what I told you yesterday," she continued. "Belle wasn't colicking at all. In fact, she ate fine the entire time you were gone. I know how worried you must have been. I really am sorry."

She felt so bad, she could hardly look at Stevie. Even though she thought lying to Stevie had been justified in this case—especially now that Stevie really was going to camp—she had never told even the whitest of white lies to Stevie before, for any reason. The night before, the image of Stevie's horror-stricken face had haunted Carole's dreams.

To Carole's amazement, Stevie grinned. "I wasn't worried at all," she assured them. "Not the slightest bit."

"But," Carole protested, puzzled, "I *told* you Belle was colicking. Colic is really serious." She felt immensely relieved that Stevie wasn't angry at her, but at the same time she wondered whether Stevie had lost her mind. Stevie was always properly concerned about her horse—why wouldn't she worry about something as scary as colic? "You looked really upset when I told you," Carole said.

"Oh, believe me, I was," Stevie replied airily. She twined her fingers through Belle's mane as she spoke. "In fact, after you left I cried for half an hour. Nice and loud. It really got to Chad."

Carole stared in amazement. Lisa began to laugh. "You mean you knew?" she asked. "You figured out what we were doing?"

"Of course," Stevie said. "It was obvious."

"I don't think it was that obvious to Chad," Lisa pointed out.

"No, of course not," Stevie replied patiently. "Nothing's obvious to a blockhead like him. But among higher life-forms such as ourselves—oh, come on, Lisa, of course I thought it was obvious. It was exactly what I would have done."

Lisa grinned. If she hadn't managed to out-Stevie Stevie, at least she'd tied her.

"It wouldn't have worked if I hadn't acted worried, too," Stevie pointed out. "If only you and Carole had seemed upset, Chad would have smelled a rat for sure."

A sudden thought made Lisa's mouth fall open. From the look on Carole's face, Lisa knew she was thinking the same thing. "Mrs. Reg!" she said.

Carole began to laugh. She laughed so hard she had to sit down. "Stevie, you would have loved it, it was unbelievable," she said between giggles. She related what Mrs. Reg had told Chad. Lisa patted Belle sadly on the neck and mimicked Mrs. Reg. " 'Poor baby, she's dying of a broken heart.' "

Stevie gave a shout, and for a moment the three of them were convulsed with laughter. "Mrs. Reg said that?" Stevie asked when she had partly recovered.

"As Carole is my witness," Lisa said. "I thought the two of us would die right there."

"You'll never know how much you owe us, Stevie," Carole said. "I had to struggle so hard not to laugh in front of Chad that I probably strained some very important muscles. I probably shortened my life by three years."

117

Stevie stroked Belle's nose thoughtfully. "But I wonder why she did it," she said. "I mean, Mrs. Reg couldn't have believed that Belle was really sick."

"Not for a moment," Lisa agreed. "She knows way too much about horses for that."

"Good thing Chad doesn't," Stevie mused. "His ignorance comes in handy sometimes."

"Plus, Mrs. Reg knew Belle had been tranquilized," Carole said thoughtfully. "She was standing in the aisle looking at the lesson chart when Judy gave Belle the injection. I'm sure she saw the whole thing."

A sudden thought occurred to Lisa. "She told that goat story," she said, her eyes growing large with amazement. "Remember, Carole? The story that seemed completely pointless but gave me the idea for our plan? She started the whole thing!"

"She couldn't have done it on purpose!" Carole protested. Mrs. Reg occasionally showed a sense of humor, but she never approved of The Saddle Club's pranks— much less encouraged them.

"Let's ask her," Stevie said. They hurriedly finished grooming Belle and put her back into her stall. Then they went into Max's office. Max and Deborah were there.

"Stevie!" Max said with an enormous, slightly mischievous grin. "Glad to see you back! How are you feeling?"

"Fine, thanks," Stevie said.

"And how is Belle?" Deborah asked, with a grin that mirrored her husband's.

"She's fine." Stevie didn't feel like going into details. She suspected from the way Max and Deborah were smiling that they knew all about poor, sick Belle and her miraculous recovery. "We're looking for Mrs. Reg."

"She's in the tack room, I think," Max said. "Are you sure you're feeling okay?"

"I'm all over my funny-bone-itis, if that's what you mean. Thanks, Max." Stevie shut the office door.

"Funny-bone-itis?" Carole asked as they walked toward the tack room.

"Inflammation of the funny bone," Lisa answered.

Stevie nodded. "It causes excessive prank-playing. I took a rest cure."

"Meaning she was grounded, so she got over it," Lisa explained.

Stevie just grinned. Mrs. Reg was indeed in the tack room, and when she saw the three girls, her face lit up in a somewhat secretive smile.

"I'm so relieved that your horse is feeling better,

Stevie," she said before they could ask her anything. "Tell me, has she developed a taste for coffee yet?"

Lisa and Carole snorted, but Stevie was confused. "No," she said. "Why would she?"

"That's good," Mrs. Reg said. "I was worried that she might start liking it."

Carole and Lisa exchanged glances and began to giggle. So Mrs. Reg knew about the coffee, too! "Mrs. Reg," Carole said, "why did you—"

Mrs. Reg held up her hand to stop her. "You think you've got problems," she said to Stevie in a serious voice. "I had four of them."

The three girls looked at each other, then back at Mrs. Reg. *Four cups of coffee?* Carole thought.

"Four what?" asked Stevie.

Mrs. Reg frowned as if it were the most obvious answer in the world. "Brothers," she said. She nodded to them and walked away.

"You know," Stevie said as they watched her go, "the longer I know Mrs. Reg, the less I understand her."

"I don't think it matters if we understand her," Lisa said. "Poor, sick Belle!"

STEVIE HAD ONE of the best trail rides of her entire life. She had never truly appreciated her wonderful horse, she thought, until she'd been forced away from her. Riding alongside Carole and Lisa in the warm summer sunshine, cantering through green woods, splashing through crystal streams—these were the best things in life. Stevie resolved to remember this the next time she felt like dismembering Chad.

After the ride she spent a long time grooming Belle and fussing over her. At last even Lisa and Carole were ready to leave. Stevie stayed another half hour, lovingly cleaning her tack. In the end she had to run home so that she wouldn't be late for dinner. Stevie didn't need any black marks on her newly cleaned slate.

"Belle's fine," she announced when they had finished saying grace and were passing the food around. "She seems entirely okay. I even rode her for a little while."

"Oh, good," Chad said with a sigh of relief. "I know she looked much better when I saw her."

Stevie's other brothers, Michael and Alex, told her how happy they were that Belle was okay. To Stevie's surprise, her parents just smiled. They didn't say anything. They didn't act worried about Belle at all. Stevie knew they didn't love Belle the way she did, but on the other hand, they paid the vet bills. "I don't think we'll need to call Judy again," Stevie assured her father.

"That's nice," he said. "Please pass the sliced tomatoes, Stevie."

Geez, Stevie thought as she passed the tomatoes, *a*

person's horse could die around here and everyone would just keep eating. She looked sideways at Chad. He was a cretin, but at least he had feelings.

After supper Stevie loaded the dishwasher while Alex cleared the table. Upstairs she could hear the light *bop-pop* noises that meant Chad was dribbling his soccer ball around his room. When she was finished in the kitchen she went up to see him.

Outside his door she paused. Chad had long ago plastered the entire thing with his bumper sticker collection, but right in the center was a brand-new sign in his handwriting: S. S. C. G. S. O.! Stevie had no trouble interpreting most of it: "Something Saddle Club Girls Stay Out!" She pushed the door open without knocking. "Does the first S stand for *slimy* or *stupid?*" she asked.

Chad stopped dribbling. "*Scurrilous,*" he said proudly.

"Wow." Stevie was impressed. "Well," she said, "I just wanted to say, like, thanks again. Like, I'm glad you don't seem too mad about being grounded."

Chad went back to dribbling. "Whatever."

"Okay." Stevie went back downstairs.

She found her parents in the living room. Her mother was reading the newspaper, and her father was lying on the couch, staring at the ceiling. "Belle really is okay," she told them again.

Her mother smiled. "We think Belle was probably okay all along," she said.

Oh, Stevie thought. *That explains why they didn't act worried—they knew it was a ruse all along.* "Oh," she said. "Then, um, why—uh, never mind." If she made her parents think about it too hard, maybe they'd change their minds and not let her go to camp after all.

Mr. Lake looked at her and winked. "What we don't understand is why Chad chose to admit his part in everything," he said. "However, we're glad he did. We were pleased all along with the way you handled your punishment, Stevie."

"We planned to let you go to camp all along, too," Mrs. Lake added. Stevie's mouth fell open. "If and only if," her mother continued, "you took responsibility for your actions, accepted your punishments with grace, and quit playing pranks on your brothers."

"Especially the prank part," Mr. Lake said.

Stevie stood in front of them awkwardly. She didn't know what to say. For a moment she felt disappointed. The Saddle Club's whole scheme had been for nothing—except, of course, for getting even with Chad. That made her feel better.

"Now that I understand how lonely Belle is without me, I'll be better behaved," she promised her parents.

"How lonely Belle is, or how lonely you are without her?" Mrs. Lake asked.

Stevie grinned. "Both," she said. She ran up the stairs to her bedroom. She had to call Lisa and Carole—camp was only three days away!

"LAST ONE DRESSED is a rotten egg!" Stevie challenged the cabin full of girls. She yanked her T-shirt over her head. The sun was streaming through the windows and screen door, and the wooden floor was smooth and cold under her feet. Their first full day at Moose Hill Riding Camp had dawned.

"Too late," said Elsa, one of the six other girls sharing their cabin. "I'm already dressed!" She pulled the top of her sleeping bag over the pillow on her bunk.

"I didn't say the first one dressed won a prize," Stevie objected. "I said the last one—besides, you've got the

alarm clock, Elsa. Of course you're the first one ready."
She grinned, remembering how, during their first trip to
Moose Hill, she and the rest of The Saddle Club had all
disliked Elsa. Now the other girl was a good friend.

"I've got the alarm clock, and I'm naturally efficient
and organized," Elsa retorted with a friendly grin.

Carole was pulling her hair into a ponytail. "No one
ever called Stevie efficient," she said.

"I don't know about that," Stevie began to argue, but
stopped when she saw how fast the others were dressing.
She pulled on her socks. "Where're my tennis shoes? I
can't find them."

"Didn't you wear them yesterday?" Lisa asked. "They
should be under your bunk."

A loud, clear bell rang across the camp. "Breakfast!"
cried one of the other girls. Elsa and the others left the
cabin. "Looks like you're the rotten egg, Stevie!" one of
them called back over her shoulder.

Stevie laughed. "I guess I should have known better
than to issue that kind of challenge before I found all my
clothes."

Carole and Lisa helped Stevie look under the bunks.
Lisa looked under Stevie's sleeping bag, too, and Carole
checked behind the door.

"I didn't wear them yesterday. I had my cowboy boots

on all day," Stevie said. "After all, we were unloading the horses and putting them in the stable."

Lisa nodded. It was important to wear sturdy shoes around horses, in case they stepped on your feet.

"Just put your boots on now," Carole suggested.

"But I really wanted my tennis shoes for breakfast," Stevie said. She rummaged through her duffel bag. "Here they are! In the outside pocket. I don't remember putting them there."

Lisa sat down on her bunk to wait for Stevie. "After all that happened last week, I still can hardly believe we're here," she said. "I'm excited about everything Prancer and I can learn this week—with your help, of course," she added thoughtfully. "One of the things I learned last week is how much like sisters the three of us are—and how lucky I am to have two such good friends."

"Just tell us if we get out of hand," Carole said softly. "We want the good parts of being sisters, but not the bad parts."

Lisa nodded. She was glad she wasn't feeling jealous of Carole anymore. She was even gladder that Carole understood. "I feel so lucky," she repeated.

Stevie tied her right shoe in a double knot and reached for her left. "I feel even luckier," she said,

thrusting her foot into the shoe. "Without you two I'd—
Ayahhhh!" She yanked her foot back out. "Ayahh! *Jelly!*
That creep put jelly in my shoe!" She waved her foot
in the air. Purple glop dripped from her toes. "I'll kill
him!"

Lisa and Carole fell over on the bunks, laughing.

"It's not funny," Stevie said. "It's completely disgusting. I am so totally grossed out." She stomped out to the
porch and shook her shoe over the railing.

"Stevie," Lisa called after her, "you left purple foot-
prints."

"Foodprints," Carole said, and they howled.

A big blob of jelly fell out of Stevie's shoe onto the
weeds in front of the cabin. Stevie lifted the tongue of
her shoe and peered inside. "There's something jammed
in the toe," she announced, coming back to the door.
When she saw the purple prints on the floor she started
to laugh, too. She removed her jelly-smeared sock and
came inside.

"So disgusting," she said, shaking her head. She sat
down next to Lisa and pulled the object out of the toe.

"It's a Baggie," Lisa said.

"With jelly all over it, and a note inside," Stevie said,
nodding. "This better be good." She gingerly opened the
little plastic bag and pulled out a piece of paper.

"It's from Chad," she announced.

Carole sat up. "What a surprise."

Stevie smoothed the paper out and read, " 'Dear Stevie, I know your horse wasn't sick. Your friends were faking all the way. Tell Carole I know garden dirt when I see it. But you shouldn't have had to miss camp, and anyway, I wanted to have a week without you bugging me. I promise not to use Super Glue again. What do you think of the jelly?' "

Lisa peeked over Stevie's shoulder. "It's signed 'Love, Chad.' "

"Oh, gag," Stevie said. "As soon as I get home, I'm going to kill him."

"He knew!" Carole shrieked. "He knew we were faking!" She couldn't believe it.

"What does he mean by garden dirt?" Stevie asked.

Carole and Lisa looked at each other. "Oh," Lisa said. "We smeared some into Belle's coat, to make it look dull."

"Unhealthy," Carole added. She looked guiltily at Stevie. "It brushed right out."

Stevie buried her head in her hands. "I can't believe he knew."

"If he knew, then why did he confess?" Lisa asked.

"It says right in the note," Carole answered. "He wanted Stevie to be able to go to camp. He's grounded now. He took a punishment for Stevie."

They looked at one another in silence. "That's really noble," Lisa said.

"Oh, double gag, it is not," Stevie said as she swiped at her jelly-covered foot with a tissue. "He's got a whole week now to sneak through my room. I bet he finds my diary and has it published in *The Willow Creek Gazette*. Plus, it's not like he didn't deserve to be punished. And he put jelly in my shoes!"

Lisa looked at the note again. "He really cares about you," she said. "I bet you really care about him, too."

"Yuck," Stevie said. She threw her tennis shoe on the floor in disgust and searched through her bag for a clean sock. She found one and put it on.

"So who really believed our plan?" Carole asked. They thought for a moment.

"No one," Stevie said at last. "I didn't, Mrs. Reg didn't, my parents didn't, and Chad didn't."

"But everyone pretended they did."

Stevie grinned. "Slick, wasn't it? And so it worked, and here I am, at Moose Hill, with Belle and the two of you!"

"And Phil," Lisa added. "And if we're going to get any breakfast at all, we've got to run."

"Phil! I forgot all about him!" Stevie tore her other shoe off and yanked her cowboy boots on. "Let's go!" She ran out the door. The others followed, laughing.

"I bet you do care about Chad," Lisa persisted as they jogged up the hill toward the dining hall. "I bet you do."

Stevie looked at her in amazement. "Of course I do! He's my brother!"

Carole laughed and shook her head. "I can't believe he knew all along," she said. "I guess I don't understand this sibling stuff at all."

ABOUT THE AUTHOR

BONNIE BRYANT is the author of many books for young readers, including novelizations of movie hits such as *Teenage Mutant Ninja Turtles* and *Honey, I Blew Up the Kid*, written under her married name, B. B. Hiller.

Ms. Bryant began writing The Saddle Club in 1986. Although she had done some riding before that, she intensified her studies then and found herself learning right along with her characters Stevie, Carole, and Lisa. She claims that they are all much better riders than she is.

Ms. Bryant was born and raised in New York City. She still lives there, in Greenwich Village, with her two sons.

Don't miss Bonnie Bryant's next exciting Saddle Club
adventure . . .

WILD HORSES
The Saddle Club #58

Lisa Atwood thinks the fancy boarding school she vis-
its for the day is nice enough. But she'd never want to
go there! It's a two-hour drive from Willow Creek,
home of her two best friends, Stevie and Carole, and
her favorite horse, Prancer. Then Lisa learns that her
mother has enrolled her in the exclusive school. Is
Lisa leaving The Saddle Club for good?